South Carolina State Library
Columbia, S.C.

Printed in the United States of America.

First Printing, 1996
Second Printing, 1998

Library of Congress Catalog Card Number: 96-96970

ISBN: 0-9654018-0-4

The short stories contained in this book are works of
fiction. Names, characters, places, and incidents are
products of the author's imagination or are used fictitiously.
Any resemblance to actual events or locales or persons,
living or dead, is entirely coincidental.

"Toy Counter Encounter" appeared in the December 1997
edition of *Back Porch* magazine.

For my granddaughters Rachel and Jessica

ACKNOWLEDGMENTS

Many people have made this book possible.

Several story ideas can be traced to my late father whose name I proudly bear. He labored hard for many years, often at low wages, as a soft-drink bottler for various bottling companies in Montgomery and Dothan, Alabama. Although my father lacked a formal education, he overcame this disability because he was smart, tough, imaginative, and possessed of a work ethic few could emulate. My father, a private, closed-mouth man and a sensitive, kind parent, could be very funny and entertaining. He loved his family and his family loved him. I miss the guy. I particularly miss his offerings of verities, my favorite being, "Don't never learn another man your job; he's liable to take it from you."

Other story ideas as well as a couple of the recipes reproduced here came from my mother, my father's greatest treasure. She is a modest, sweet, pretty woman. She is also very bright and fitted, as she has pointedly reminded me on occasion, with "walking-around sense." For much of her life, she was employed as a retail sales clerk who sold women's clothing. Her customers list was the envy of the other clerks at every store in which she worked. During the

Second World War, she briefly worked at a local hospital as a Red Cross nurse's aid. Her more difficult years were when she stayed at home to care for my sister, my brother, and me. Whether she worked outside or inside the home, however, she prepared the meals for the five of us, for a long time on a smelly, kerosene stove; she washed our clothes, for several years on her knees, bent over a bathtub and using a scrub board;[1] she ironed our clothes, many of which she made

---

[1]   After World War II ended and new washing machines became available once more, my father brought home to my mother a used, wringer-type washing machine. Until the bathroom could be wired and plumbed to accommodate the machine, my parents kept the appliance on the front porch. It remained there for several weeks as they waited for an electrician and a plumber to come install it. Because so many passers-by came up onto the porch and knocked on the front door to inquire about the machine, my father put up a sign that read, "This Washing Machine Is Not For Sale." My mother made him take the sign down, saying she'd rather have people think she wanted to sell the machine than have them think she intended to keep it on the porch.

One other memory associated with the washing machine concerns my brother. Under orders from our mother to shell a sack of blackeyed peas by noon, my brother, anxious to join the other kids in playing rubber guns, attempted to use the wringer on the washing machine to shell the peas. He inserted several pods into the wringer, fully anticipating the pressure applied by the rollers onto the pods would cause the peas to pop out into a bowl he had placed on the wringer's opposite side. The rollers, of course, simply flattened the pods and the peas. More seriously, the

herself from sugar sacks that my father brought home from work; she disciplined us, my father included, whenever we needed it, which was, in the case of my brother and me, fairly often; she nursed and treated us when we were sick or injured; and she always, always prayed for us, sometimes with a heart that ached and with eyes filled with tears. I cannot read verses twenty-five through thirty-one of the thirty-first chapter of *Proverbs* without thinking immediately of her. The author must have had my mother in mind when these words were written.

Except for the recipe for boiled peanuts, which my colleague Bill Howell gave me, the other recipes were supplied by my wife Prue, including that of her mother's recipe for War Fruitcake. Although Prue worked as a college librarian during most of our marriage, she managed nonetheless to become one of South Carolina's best cooks.

---

squashing of the pods and peas left green stains on the washing machine's rollers. When our mother saw the stained rollers, she demanded an explanation from my brother. He told her, "I was just trying to hurry and get through so I could go play rubber guns with Punk and them." She responded, "I'll rubber gun you, if you don't get that stain off and get those peas shelled. He got the stain off. He got the peas shelled.

Aside from cooking and providing financial support, Prue has given our son, who is a Charleston doctor, and me other, more valuable gifts. Indeed, much of the credit for whatever success our son and I enjoy, we both owe to the steady, quiet support given unselfishly and lovingly by her to us. Throughout our years together, she has faithfully followed Paul's counsel in *Colossians*, chapter three, verse twelve, all the while willingly sacrificing for our son and me and consistently putting our interests ahead of her own.

Editing suggestions and encouragement came from several dear friends who read the manuscript or parts of it: Alex Sanders, Bill Howell, whom I've mentioned earlier, Mary Au, Bob Cook, Jasper Cureton, Peg Fox, Ginger Goforth, Debbie Hottel, Righton McCallum, Travis Medlock, and Lauri Soles.

C.T.G., Jr.

CONTENTS

SWEET POTATO
BISCUITS

Ruby Mallard drained the last of the kerosene from the red and gray can into the round glass jug that held the stove's clear fuel. "You know one thing?" she said to her next-door neighbor Lena Strickland as she put the kerosene can down on the floor by the back door and lit the oven, "I hate fall. I just hate it."

"You hate fall? Why would anybody hate fall?" Lena asked, laughing.

"That durn fair, that's why. It comes every fall, and it's here already. I just can't stand the stupid thing." She leaned against the sink, turned on the water, reached for a bar of yellow soap that lay on the window sill, and began washing her hands.

"But, Ruby, your boys love it. And you know you and Hester'll have to take them out there."

"Yeah, I expect you're right," Ruby complained, drying her hands on her apron. She lifted the lid to the flour container and scooped up some flour. To the flour, she added baking soda and sugar and sifted the three ingredients into a mixing bowl. "I'll tell you, I don't feel safe out there, what with all them peculiar-looking people the fair brings with it and the awful things you hear about them."

Ruby peeled two medium-sized, baked sweet potatoes, dropped them into the bowl, and combined the orange lumps with the dry ingredients. "I guess it wouldn't be so bad and I probably wouldn't mind going out there and hate it so much, but every year the boys or Hester one'll do something to upset me."

"Like what?" Lena asked, laughing again.

"Well, take last year. We weren't inside the gate good when Wendell and Byron, they go over to this place where for a nickel you get to throw two baseballs at three wood milk bottles. You know, it's the one where, if you knock down all three bottles, they give you a goldfish in a jar full of water."

Lena nodded.

"Now Wendell," Ruby said, continuing, "he can't hit nothing." She paused again, and with an admiring tone, said, "But Byron, little as he is to be eight years old, he can knock the wings off a yellow jacket twenty feet away."

Ruby cut a small amount of lard into her sweet potato mixture and then walked from the table to the ice box. She opened a door, removed a bottle of buttermilk, and returned to her mixing bowl. She poured a tiny bit into the bowl, mixing it with the other contents and making a dough. "Poor Wendell, he can't hit nothing. So what does he do? He spends all his money the first ten minutes we're there. Every penny he has he spends, trying to win one of them goldfish. Heck, he couldn't knock over one bottle, much less three. Byron, he won a goldfish the first time he tried, which made Wendell want to win one that much worse. He can't stand to have his little brother show him up."

Ruby took the dough from the bowl and placed it onto a board she had lightly sprinkled with flour. After folding, pressing, and stretching the dough, she flattened it into a half-inch-thick disc, cut the disc into silver dollar-sized circles, and placed the cut-outs onto a greased baking sheet. "Anyway, after Byron won his goldfish—and gave it to me to carry for him all night long—we stood there and watched Wendell literally throw his money away," Ruby grumbled. "For the rest of the night, Wendell didn't have no money to do nothing with. He couldn't ride nothing. He couldn't buy nothing to eat. He couldn't play no more games. He couldn't go in the side shows. And when Hester wouldn't give him another thirty-five cents, he squalled and pitched a fit. I've never been more miserable in all my born days, I don't believe."

"Just because Wendell was crying?"

"No. Lord knows, that was bad enough," Ruby said. "But let me ask you this. How would you like walking around and having to carry a jar full of cold water that's got a fish in it, which you know'll be dead before you leave to go home? The water is sloshing all over you, wetting your clothes, freezing your hands. And as plumb miserable as that makes you, you also gotta listen to a crying young'un. I'm telling you, I can't go through with that again this year."

Ruby slid the biscuits into the 450-degree oven. She wiped her hands on her apron and sighed. "And, of course, Byron, he started squalling, too. His darn old goldfish died, just like I knew it would. All of a sudden, it just floated up to the top of the jar and flipped over on its back. I think he thought I killed it to get out of carrying it. Maybe, just maybe, I can talk them out of going there this year."

On the way to the fairgrounds, Ruby thought about her failure to talk the males in her life out of going to the fair. Her husband suggested she should stay home if she really didn't enjoy going. But somebody'd have to go and look after Hester and the boys. After all, what if something happened?

No sooner had they walked through the turnstile than the two boys took off running toward the midway's lights, music, noise, and thrills. They ran about thirty yards, turned around, and doubled back when they heard their father yell after them, "Didn't y'all forget something?"

Hester reached into his back pocket and pull out his wallet. He gave each son a dollar. The boys started to dart away, but Ruby stopped them.

"Wendell," Ruby said, "like I told you before we left the house, I'm putting you in charge of your little brother. Y'all are not, I repeat, not to eat anything unless it comes from a church booth."

"Oh, Mama," cried Wendell "don't no churches sell cotton candy."

"Okay, y'all can buy cotton candy from the fair people, but that's all."

"Yessum."

"This year, y'all stay away from them old games. All they want to do is take your money away from you."

"Uh-huh," Wendell said anxiously, looking away from his mother and toward the fun beyond his mother's back. Byron pulled on his sleeve, wanting to go.

"Y'all can go in the freak shows and the House of Mirrors, but be careful in it," Ruby admonished. "Y'all can ride the Ferris wheel, the merry-go-round . . . "

"The merry-go-round?" Wendell whined. "Mama, I ain't rode no merry-go-round since I was in the first grade."

"Stay off the flying swings," Ruby said, ignoring Wendell's remark. "Remember how your daddy rode it last year and got sick and threw up all over everybody? Also, be careful who y'all talk to. Watch out for strangers, especially them fair people. I wouldn't want them to steal one of y'all and sell you to somebody way off in Egypt or someplace. Your daddy and me'll be over at the Sanders Building looking at the exhibits or eating a pronto pup at St. Mark's if y'all need us for anything. Otherwise, we'll meet y'all out in front of the grandstand at six o'clock. Don't make me and your daddy have to come looking for y'all. You hear me, Wendell?"

"Yessum."

"You hear me, Byron?" Ruby asked as she squatted down and studied Byron's pretty face while awaiting his answer. Byron continued to pull at his brother's sleeve and appeared not to have heard a word his mother had said. Ruby put her hand on top of his blond head and twisted one of his many curls around her right index finger. Often, whenever she looked at her younger son, she recalled the words from *Solomon's Song*, "His mouth is most sweet: yea, he is altogether lovely. This is my beloved . . . ."

"Byron, do you hear me?" she repeated. "Look at me."

"Yessum. I heard you," Byron said, impatient to get going. "Come on, Wendell, let's find that man you told me you saw last year."

"Which one?" Wendell asked.

"The one you said had four legs and two butts."

The boys raced off, stopping at a nearby gambling stall where they handed the operator their dollar bills. He gave each boy back his change and two baseballs to throw at wooden, bottle-shaped figures. Wendell quickly threw his two, missing both times.

"Hester," Ruby said, "will you look at where they went? Will you just look at them? Tell me this, what good did it do for me to talk to them?"

"None, I don't reckon," he replied. "Come on, let's go over yonder and look at the hogs before Byron gives you a goldfish to carry."

"I don't care nothing about looking at some old hogs. I had to slop enough of them when I was growing up. Let's go over to St. Marks and get us a pronto pup or some french fries. That's where we told them we'd be anyway, either there or at the Sanders Building."

A familiar cry pierced Ruby's ears as she and Hester strolled around a glass cabinet that showcased the winners of blue ribbons in crochet and needlepoint. Ruby turned her head in the direction of Wendell's distressed voice.

"Mama! Mama! Byron's gone!" Wendell screamed.

"What? What'd you say?" Ruby exclaimed.

Wendell ran to her and threw his arms around her waist and leaned his head into her stomach. "I went over to where this man was guessing people's ages . . . "

"Slow down, won't you? And look at me," Ruby said.

"And when I turned around, Byron, he was gone," Wendell said. He began sobbing. "I'm sorry, Mama. I couldn't help it. It ain't my fault. Somebody must've grabbed him or something. I've been looking everywhere for him and when I couldn't find him I come looking for y'all."

"Oh, Lord. I knew we shouldn't have come out here. I just knew it. But no, everybody wanted to come,"

Ruby moaned. "Wendell, are you sure you looked for him good?"

"Yes, ma'am. I looked everywhere," Wendell said.

"Somebody's grabbed him for sure," Ruby speculated. "I declare. I just declare. Hester, you go to the message center right next to the front gate while me and Wendell go look for the police."

Hester hurried away as Ruby and Wendell began their hunt for a policeman. "Ain't never one around when you need them," she said.

While Ruby and Wendell searched for a policeman, a dispassionate voice boomed over the public address system. "Byron Mallard. Byron Mallard. Meet your daddy in front of the grandstand. Byron Mallard. Byron Mallard. Please meet your daddy in front of the grandstand."

The announcement ran several more times before Ruby caught up with a deputy sheriff. She and Wendell quickly explained about Byron. The deputy contacted another deputy. They joined Hester at the grandstand. Byron had not responded to the announcement.

"Mrs. Mallard," the first deputy said, "you go with Deputy Moss here and y'all check out all them side shows. I'll go with Wendell and we'll do the concession stands, things like that. Mr. Mallard, you go take a look at the rides. We'll meet back here in thirty minutes. If we ain't found him by then, then we'll call the sheriff about us going and searching all them trailers back over yonder. Them fair people ain't going to like it none, if we have to do that."

"Well, I've heard tales they'll snatch away little children and sell them," Ruby said. "Don't you think we ought call the sheriff right now?"

"No, ma'am, I don't," the deputy snapped. "Come on, Wendell."

Ruby and Deputy Moss zipped in and out of one side show after another. No Byron. Not even a Byron look-a-like.

"Ma'am, I don't think it's any need to look in them hoochy-koochy shows for your boy," the deputy said. "You gotta be sixteen to get in them. What kinda show you reckon he liked anyhow?"

"He was talking about trying to find the show that had the man with four legs and two . . . . The man with four legs."

"Oh. That's the show what's got all them freaks, the Bubble Face Man, the Human Camel—heck, my brother-in-law's got a hump and you can see him for nothing." Ruby was not amused. "They also got a giant and some midgets in there," he added.

The two walked past the ticket taker to the rear of the spectator area beneath the tent. A comic wedding that featured people and property in miniature occupied the stage at the moment. A heavily veiled bride concluded her march toward the groom and the other members of the diminutive wedding party. "That kinda looks like him, Mr. Moss, over there, sitting on the fourth row up, close to this end," Ruby said, with hope in her voice.

As they eased their way toward the small body packed in with others on the fourth row, the minister asked the bride and groom to repeat their vows. The mother of the bride wailed, as did the father who pretended to read a large piece of paper that he displayed to the audience. Printed in huge letters at the top of the paper were the words "Wedding Expenses." Finally, Ruby reached a spot where she could see more clearly the person she thought might be her son. Her heart sank. It was not Byron.

The little minister, played by Toy Land, the show's star and manager, pronounced the couple who stood before him husband and wife. Smiling, he told the groom, "You may now kiss the bride."

The groom reached out to lift the veil, but the bride angrily pushed him back. "He ain't kissing me. Nobody told me I had to do that."

The voice belonged to Byron.

✤

Toy Land faced Ruby. His chin rested against his chest, his head hung so low. "Mrs. Mallard," he explained, "the young lady who usually plays the bride lost a filling and had to go to the dentist, it was hurting her so bad. Anyhow, I saw your son, as pretty a child as I ever saw, and asked him if he'd like to make an easy five dollars and he asked me how and I told him. I also told him he'd have to wear a dress and walk out on the stage when the piano player started playing 'Here Comes the Bride' and all he'd have to say would be yes to the questions I'd be asking him. I told him it wouldn't take him no more than thirty minutes at most and he wouldn't have to do it but once, at the five o'clock show. I felt Minnie'd be back before the one at six."

"Why didn't you try to find out where I was?" Ruby asked. "I thought somebody had kidnaped him or something."

"I wasn't thinking about that. I was worried about the show going on, disappointing people. I'm sorry. You're right, I should've tried to find you," Toy said, dropping his head.

An uncomfortable silence followed.

"I'll tell you something, though. And I'm not excusing what I did. You know, Byron's got five dollars which he didn't have an hour ago. I expect it'll be gone in another hour, once he gets out of that dress and back outside. But, he's got something else, something nobody can ever take from him."

"And what's that?" Ruby asked, still upset with the tiny man who wore the costume of a nineteenth century parson.

"Mrs. Mallard, he's now got a special memory. All his life he'll remember his performance this afternoon. When he's an old man like me, he can tell his grandchildren, 'You know, one day at the fair I was in a play with the famous Toy Land and a bunch of other little people and I got paid five dollars for it.'" He extended his wee right hand.

"Again, I'm sorry to have upset you. I didn't mean you or him any harm. That's the God's truth."

Ruby, touched by his words and his sincerity, took his hand and tenderly cupped hers around it. "Reverend, I mean . . ."

"Just call me Toy."

"You needn't apologize," she said, smiling. "Let me ask you, do you know anything about sweet potato biscuits?"

"No, ma'am. Can't say I do."

"When you look at sweet potato biscuits, they don't look like they'd be any good. They don't look like other biscuits. They're yellow or orange. They don't rise much. They're peculiar looking, different. But when you bite into one, you find out how good sweet potato biscuits really are. Up until this happened, I can't say I actually knew anything about people like y'all. Now, I know y'all are like sweet potato biscuits. Thank you for letting me and Byron bite into you."

She helped Byron remove the wedding gown and then led him to the opening at the rear of the tent. "Toy."

"Ma'am?"

"His grandchildren'll think he made it all up."

Mary Goolsby's Recipe for Sweet Potato Biscuits

2 c. self-rising flour (or more as needed)
1/4 t. baking soda
2 T. sugar
4 T. shortening
2 T. buttermilk
2 c. mashed, baked sweet potatoes

Sift the dry ingredients together and add to the mashed sweet potatoes. Cut in the shortening and buttermilk to make a light dough, mixing like regular biscuits. Roll the dough out and cut and place on a greased cookie sheet. Bake in a 450-degree oven for about ten minutes or until they are golden brown. Butter and serve hot.

Serves: Four to six persons (provided no one is greedy).

Note: Sweet potato biscuits do not rise as much as regular biscuits.

GRANDPA'S BODY

Alto Peacock's large hands gripped the corners of the table as he sat, facing his wife and two children on the other side. "Well, one thing's for sure. I can't afford no undertaker."

"But, Pa, we can't just let him stay in yonder. We gotta get him funeralized and all," Favor, his older child, cried.

"Funeralized? What with? Y'all ain't heard a thing I been saying. This ain't getting me no place, talking to y'all. It ain't getting me no place at all," Alto moaned. He stood, trudged over to the trash burner, and turned his huge rear toward its hot surface. "Heckfire, I gotta take y'all to church this morning, too. I ain't been to church in so long I've done near forgot when I last went. I bet it's been a hundred years." Alto, Jr., who had been loading a piece of buttered light bread with fig preserves, looked up at his father. "Why you gotta do that for, Pa?"

"'Cause your grandpa's made me promise him, that's why. Last night, just before he died, he said to me, 'Alto.' And I said, 'What?' He said, 'I want you to promise me something.' I said, 'What?' And he said, 'I want you to promise me you'll take the young'uns to church after I die.' Now, what kind of fool promise is that for a dying man to ask somebody to make anyhow? I don't want to go to no church."

Sarajean, whose father lay dead in the next room, raised her head from her hands. "I think he wanted y'all to pray for him, Alto, to pray for his soul," she said softly.

"I ain't got no time to go to no church and pray for nobody. I gotta figure out what to do with his corpse. Don't you understand? Favor's right. We can't just leave him in there. It ain't like he's a dog or cat what got run over. We can't just dig a hole and throw him in it, you know."

"Alto," she frowned, "it ain't your problem nohow. It's mine. So, why don't y'all just go on to church like you promised my daddy. Go on to the one up the street and leave me here to study on this thing a spell. You young'uns, y'all hurry and go put your good clothes on and bundle up good. It's cold outside."

The three, with Alto in front, walked single-file the six blocks to the Appletree Street Methodist Church. They went inside. The service had already started.

After awhile, the crimson-faced, white-haired preacher took the pulpit from the song leader. "Take out your pew Bibles, if you will and follow me while I read from *Matthew* the twenty-fifth chapter, verses thirty-four through forty-six." In a grave voice, the preacher read Jesus' admonition to welcome, feed, and clothe the poor and the sick—or face the consequences.

When the preacher finished reading, Alto leaned down and muttered to Favor, "Did you hear what he just read?"

Favor nodded affirmatively.

"This here, child, just might be our lucky day."

For almost an hour, the man behind the pulpit, slapping his Bible and shouting until he was almost hoarse, warned the churchgoers that they were in danger of hellfire and damnation if they failed to help the poor and the sick. With each warning of the doom that was sure to follow if they did not do so, Alto sat higher in his seat, figuring.

At last, the sermon ended, its deliverer nearly spent. "Now," he said tiredly, "as I close, I want every one of you to think about how you're spending your money. Are you spending everything you earn on the things of this world, namely things for yourself, or are you investing in the world to come? Are you spending some of your money on those who need it? What have you given lately to the poor of our community? What have you given lately to the poor of this state and nation?"

An altar call followed. Alto directed his children into the aisle while the congregation sang a Fanny Crosby hymn. He lumbered to the altar, his children behind him, and fell weeping into the waiting arms of the preacher, who hugged all three.

The congregation continued to sing the invitational hymn as Alto and the preacher conversed with each other. Alto did most of the talking.

"My friends," the preacher began, once the singing stopped, "we have with us this morning Brother Alto Peacock and his children, Favor and Alto, Jr. Brother Peacock tells me this is the first time in years he's been inside a church. He tells me, too, this is the very first time his children have ever been to church and he's mighty ashamed of it and wants God's forgiveness. He also tells me that he and his family have a great need, indeed, an immediate need, and he thinks that's why they were led here this morning. Just last night, his wife's daddy, the grandfather of these two precious children here, up and died but only after making Brother Peacock promise to take them to church with him this morning. Any church. And they chose ours. Brother Peacock hasn't called the funeral home to come pick up the body because he says he hasn't got any money to pay for an undertaker."

"That's the truth," Alto affirmed, tears streaming down both cheeks, his lips quivering. The two children nodded also.

"He can't afford a casket," the preacher continued. "He can't afford a cemetery lot or a grave marker. Right this minute, his father-in-law's body is there at Brother Peacock's house and they don't know what to do. He says he can't just dig a hole and throw him in it. I think y'all agree with me that these folks have got a problem, a real serious problem."

Churchgoers looked at one another, most murmuring to those around them and nearly all craning their necks to get a better look at Brother Peacock and his children.

"I agree with Brother Peacock, it's like the Lord sent him and his children to us, to test us, to challenge our faith. I look on this as an opportunity for each of us to invest in the kingdom that is to come."

The preacher stepped beside the communion table on which he had earlier placed the offering. "I know we've already taken the offering one time this morning, but I'm going to ask the ushers to come forward again. I want them to empty the offering plates and pass them around one more time. Won't you please give something? Won't you put your money where your faith is? If you'll do that, I'll guarantee you, God will bless you for it."

Alto and the children left the church after the preacher told Alto that he felt the special offering had produced enough to pay his father-in-law's funeral expenses. What pleased Alto even more, however, was the preacher's statement that there might even be some money left over for Alto, but he would let Alto know for sure after he paid the funeral home. Meanwhile, the preacher would call the funeral home. Alto relished his good fortune and the prospect of a bonus.

As Alto came within sight of his house, he saw a long, dark vehicle pull away from the curb. He marveled at how quickly the church had gotten things moving and about how wonderful it was that he would be getting anything left over.

Sarajean remained at the curb, watching the black vehicle carry her daddy away. After it disappeared from view, she turned to go back into the house. Seeing Alto and the children, she stopped. Alto, his face anchored by a grin, asked, "Which funeral home come and got your pa?"

"Didn't neither one," she said, "that was the medical school. I done give Daddy over to medical science."

Mary Goolsby's Recipe for Fig Preserves

3 c. ripe figs
2 c. sugar

Wash the figs and cut off the stems. Put the figs in a stainless steel pot and cover them with the sugar. Let the figs and sugar stand overnight or for twelve hours. Bring the figs and sugar to a boil and cook over a low heat, being careful not to burn the figs. Simmer the figs until they are syrupy. Afterward, ladle the figs into hot, sterile jars. Leave an approximate 1/4-inch headspace and cover the preserves at once with metal lids. Make certain the lid bands are tight and then bathe the jars in boiling water for 30 minutes.

Serves: One plus persons (occasionally, a person will consume an entire jar without passing it on to others around the table).

TOY COUNTER

ENCOUNTER

We left the picture show that Saturday after watching a cowboy hero and his funny sidekick each shoot his six-shooter at bad guys more than eighty times without reloading, a gang of wisecracking New York City teenagers avoid yet another day of school and bring criminals to justice, cartoon characters gayly assault each other with explosives, shotgun blasts, and blows to the head, and a drugged, securely bound masked man encased in concrete inside an exploding munitions ship surely die (with his mask on and his identity thus preserved) before he could wake up, free himself, and swim to safety twenty-five miles away. As I paused for my eyes to adjust to the daylight, I glimpsed my short, box-shaped, tow-headed little brother dart across the street and run straight for the dime store.

He dodged past two farmers clad in bib overalls and hunkered down on the sidewalk, munching boiled peanuts from small, damp brown sacks. Empty hulls encircled their brogans. They appeared not to notice my brother, although he nearly knocked one of them over. Both men seemed dazzled by a street preacher who screamed passages from *The Revelation* to all sinners within earshot.

"'And upon her forehead was a name written, MYSTERY,'" I heard him yell as my brother caught the revolving door and pushed his way inside. I overtook him moments later, having raced by the two farmers and the preacher. I found my brother exactly where I knew he would be—at the toy counter.

A toy counter to my brother was like a church altar. When standing before one of these holy tables, he never failed to practice the ancient ritual of the laying-on-of-hands. He attempted to bless every toy within reach.

To this day, I've not seen another store clerk like her. If God indeed makes us what we are, God certainly did a good job with her. She was perfect for the toy counter. She stood at least six feet tall and must have weighed more than two hundred pounds. The black clothes she always wore made me hesitate more than once to look at the toys on display. I never saw her smile and I never heard her thank a kid for buying a toy. She'd make kids stand there a long time before she would wait on them. And if they didn't have the right change, she'd complain about it. She didn't like a lot of pennies either.

But what made her perfect for the toy counter, though, were the dark glasses she always wore. I never quite knew where she was looking or whom she was watching. Sometimes when I thought she was looking straight ahead, she'd really be looking to her left.

Many a time a kid would come up to the counter and, after glancing at where she was posted and being satisfied she was looking the other way, would pick up a toy and start playing with it only to be hollered at and told to put that toy down unless "you're gonna to buy it." She had a way of catching a kid off guard.

My brother, conscious of the baleful form on the other side but never appreciating the problem posed by the dark glasses, ran up to the toy counter to see what new delights it contained. His blue eyes barely cleared the top of the counter. He quickly spotted a yellow and blue toy he had not seen the weekend before. He peered up at the grave guardian looming nearby and concluded she was looking elsewhere. "Look," he whispered to me, "a motorcycle policeman."

He peeked at the somber shape one more time and, believing everything was still safe, slowly reached and picked up the motorcycle with the blue cop astride its yellow frame. "Plpplpplpplp'un," he intoned softly, imitating the sound of a motorcycle as he rolled the toy on the counter top in an imaginary chase of bad guys. "Plpplpplpplp'un," he intoned more loudly.

Suddenly, a large hand slammed his tiny fingers and the toy they held against a glass divider on the counter. The glass broke and sliced the little finger on his right hand. He shrieked as he dropped the motorcycle. Blood oozed from the cut. The powerful steward, who until she saw the blood was smiling for having scored a direct hit, swooned and fell onto the toy counter, collapsing displays and smashing toys beneath her massive frame.

On seeing my brother bleed, I began to cry. The cut was not all that serious, but blood is blood and I was scared of blood. The manager came up and took my brother to the water fountain and set him down on the platform children stood upon to reach the water. He wet his handkerchief and wiped the blood from my brother's finger, telling him everything would be okay.

Meanwhile, somebody lifted the heavy figure from the counter, brought her around, and led her to a back room.

After awhile, my brother's finger quit bleeding. The man then poured alcohol on the cut. This made my brother howl again. The man told my brother it wouldn't burn long and it didn't. A clerk produced a Band-Aid and the man put it over the cut. My brother soon quieted down.

As we started to leave, the huge malevolent form reappeared from the back room. She trudged over to the toy counter and picked up something. She then came to where my brother sat and knelt down beside him. "Here, boy," she said, holding the blood-stained motorcycle out to him. "You want this. You can have it."

My brother gleefully took the toy from her and immediately forgot all about his injury.

We skipped out of the store, passing by the peanut-eating squatters with the brogans and by the screaming street preacher whose voice had grown hoarse. "And I saw the woman drunken with the blood of the saints . . . ," he rasped.

"I bet you won't go back in there next Saturday and play with any more of their toys," I said to my brother.

"Why come?" he responded. "She might hit me again and then they'd give me another one of these." He rolled the motorcycle's wheels on the palm of the injured hand. "Plpplpplpplp'un. Plpplpplpplp'un."

His hope to earn another motorcycle through pain and suffering totally disappeared when we returned the following Saturday to find the toy counter no longer defended by the threatening form with the dark glasses but by a younger, more familiar menace. "Don't even look like you want to touch one," our teenage sister snarled at my brother on her first day at work.

William Howell's Recipe for Boiled Peanuts

3 qt. green peanuts
4 qt. water
1 c. salt

Place the green peanuts in their hulls into a pot of water. Cover the peanuts with water and then with the salt. Boil the peanuts for two hours, stirring occasionally. Sample the peanuts to determine whether they are done. When the peanuts are done, turn off the heat and allow the peanuts to soak in the brine until they are salty enough for your taste. (Adding more salt to the brine may sometimes be needed, depending on taste.)

Serves: Three or four people (depending on their fondness for boiled peanuts or on whether they've had anything else to eat).

A WORTHLESS
CHECK

*A*s the reflections of the Dixie Water Bottling Plant disappeared from his sideview mirrors, Milely Lassiter shivered. No one could sell soft drinks on a day like this one. Too cold. Too wet. Unseasonably so. He dreaded his first stop, Jackson's Store. Lassiter doubted he'd sell anything there, regardless of the bad weather. Ray Lee Jackson, the store's operator, hadn't bought any drinks from him since Jackson had given him a check three weeks before, a check the bank kept returning to Lassiter unpaid because of insufficient funds. Well, Lassiter decided, he didn't care if he sold the store any drinks or not. He just wanted his money. He hated having to keep asking for it.

The wipers slapped back and forth, barely clearing the rain that fell against the outside glass. A haze crept across the inside glass, prompting Lassiter to make a viewing area with his right hand as he steered with his left.

The truck, laden fully with soft drinks, struggled to pull its clinking cargo down the slick, wet highway toward Jackson's Store.

Lassiter reached the store about fifteen or twenty minutes after leaving the plant. He stopped his truck as close to the overhang as he could. He opened the door, dropped to the ground, and slammed the door behind him. With his metal-covered route book in hand, Lassiter ran to the front door of the store, opened it, and raced inside.

The storekeeper stood huddled with another man next to a potbellied stove near the back wall. On the wall hung a calender that advertised a local funeral home. The calender featured a picture of Jesus on his knees, washing the feet of a disciple. Below the picture appeared the words,

"And as ye would that men should do to you, do ye also to them likewise."

Jackson looked at Lassiter as Lassiter shut the door and hurried in. "Don't need no Dixie Water," Jackson called out before Lassiter could say anything.

"Sir?" Lassiter said, walking over to the stove, his arms outstretched and his palms pointed forward.

"I said I don't need none."

"Oh, that's okay," Lassiter said. The two men moved apart a little as Lassiter drew nearer. "Can't say I blame you none. I wouldn't buy anything today either, the weather like it is. You mind if I stand by your stove a second?"

"Help yourself. This old stove'll warm three fannies as good as it'll do two."

"Thank you," he said, facing the two men and the stove and his hands opened to capture some heat. Lassiter stood silently in front of the stove for a moment and then turned around to warm his backside. "Mr. Jackson," he said, looking his way, "could I asked you about something, please sir?"

"Go ahead. Shoot."

"You remember that check you gave me a couple of weeks ago or so?"

Jackson nodded, "Yeah. What about it?" He spit on the stove. The stove sizzled.

"Well, the bank keeps sending it back to me."

"Naw. You don't say." He spit again.

"Yes, sir. Anyhow, I was wondering if could you let me have the money instead and let me give you the check back? They're holding me responsible for it down at the plant and I just can't afford to be out of no thirty-five dollars. That's a lot of money to me. I've got your check right here," Lassiter said, patting his right back pocket.

"I'd love to oblige you, boy, but to tell the truth I'm a little short myself," Jackson said. Lassiter thought he saw Jackson wink at the other man whom Jackson once had introduced as his night man.

"Yes, sir, I'd love to oblige you. I really would."
Jackson paused, as if in thought. "I'll tell you what, you just
keep sending it back to the bank. I expect they'll pay it some
day. What you think, Titus, you think they'll pay it some
day?"

"Well, they might. Then again they might not,"
Titus said.

Jackson and Titus both laughed. They were still
laughing when Lassiter left to rejoin the bad weather.
Lassiter sat for a moment in his truck, pondering what to do.
Ain't but one thing to do, he decided, *and that's go to the
magistrate and swear out a warrant, just like the sales
manager suggested I do. And cross Jackson's Store off the
route. It doesn't do any good to sell if you can't collect on
what you sell.* He cranked the truck and drove off.

The magistrate, a druggist, listened to Lassiter's story about
the check while he waited on customers. "You got the check
with you, son?" he inquired.

Lassiter reached for his billfold and withdrew the check. He handed it to the magistrate. The magistrate studied the check for a moment.

"You say Jackson gave you the check on Monday, March 31?"

"Yes, sir," Lassiter answered.

"You're quite sure it was the thirty-first?"

"Yes, sir. I am."

"Then I'm afraid there's nothing I can do for you. This check's dated April 1, April Fool's Day."

"Does that make a difference? I mean, it being April Fool's Day? Does that make it some kind of joke or something?" Lassiter asked, incredulously.

"The fact it was April Fool's Day isn't the problem. The problem is the check is what we call a post-dated check. Under our law, a post-dated check isn't a fraudulent check."

"But he gave it to me and the bank says he didn't have enough money to pay it with. Ain't that fraud or something?"

"Our supreme court says it isn't. I'm sorry. There's really nothing that can be done about this, as a practical matter. It wouldn't do any good to sue him. He probably hasn't got anything worth levying on and by the time you paid the lawyer and all you'd be worse off than you are now. If I was you, I'd just forget the whole thing and not sell him anything anymore."

The magistrate turned to greet a customer who handed him a prescription. "Morning, Mrs. Hawkins," he said dismissing Lassiter.

After making a telephone call, Lassiter left the drug store and resumed his route. He headed for the Nickel Jamboree, the only store to which he expected to sell more than a few cases of soft drinks that day.

On his way back to the plant that evening, Lassiter stopped again at Jackson's Store and parked his truck along the shoulder of the highway. He followed into the store an attractive young woman who had parked her Studebaker beneath the overhang just as he switched off the truck's engine.

The man behind the counter looked up from his paper and pushed to one side a saucer that held a slice of fruitcake off which he had pinched several bite-size pieces. "Howdy do, young lady. Can I help you?" he asked.

"I sure hope so," the woman said, opening her purse and withdrawing a piece of paper.

"Titus, is Mr. Jackson in?" Lassiter interrupted. "I'd like to talk with him again about this check." He took the check from his wallet and offered it to Titus.

"I'll be with you in a jiffy. Customers first, you know," Titus said, rejecting Lassister's offer of the check. He smiled broadly at the pretty shopper. "What can I help you with, please ma'am?"

The woman read out a list of the things she required. As she read an item off, Titus went to a shelf, got the item, and put it on the counter.

While Titus waited on the woman, Lassiter warmed himself by the stove. His eyes caught the calendar. He read the scripture beneath the picture.

When the woman completed her shopping, Titus totaled her bill on the back of a brown sack. "If my figures're right, you owe thirty-four dollars and twelve cents."

The woman pulled a checkbook from her handbag. "Do you call this Jackson's Grocery?" she asked.

"Or Jackson's Store, either one. It don't make no never mind."

The woman wrote Jackson's Store on the check, wrote in words and figures the amount of thirty-four dollars and twelve cents, signed her correct name, and dated the check. She handed Titus her driver's license.

Titus looked at it and wrote down the woman's address on the check. He asked the woman for her telephone number, which she gave him.

"Do you mind helping me get these to my car?" she asked.

"No, ma'am. I'd be glad to help you," he said. He picked up two bags. The woman carried the other.

"Here," Lassiter said, walking quickly from the stove toward the front of the store. "I'll get the door for y'all." Titus and the woman stepped through the door and down to the car. After Titus placed the groceries onto the back seat of the woman's car, she thanked him, told him goodbye, and drove away.

Titus went back into the store. "Mr. Jackson, he ain't here," he said to Lassiter who stood again by the stove.

"I didn't think he was," Lassiter replied.

"I'll tell him you come by, though. What's your name again? I forget."

"Never mind. Thanks anyway."

As Lassiter walked toward the door, he glanced once more at the picture of Jesus and re-read the scripture below. He paused briefly, studying it. *A hard rule to follow*, he concluded. He walked out the store, got into his truck, and drove away.

Titus picked up the check left by the woman and opened the cash drawer. He put the check inside, closed the drawer, and went back to his paper and fruitcake. He failed to notice the woman, who signed her last name as Lassiter, had dated the check for the following day.

Eugenia Fraser's Recipe for War Fruitcake

4 ½ c. sifted plain flour
4 level t. baking soda
2 ½ c. applesauce
2/3 c. sugar
1 c. butter (½ lb. or 2 sticks)
1 egg
1 lb. raisins
1 pkg. dried dates
1 pkg. dried figs
3/4 lb. candied pineapple
2/3 lb. candied cherries
3/4 lb. citron
½ lb. almonds
3/4 lb. English walnuts
1 t. cinnamon
1 t. nutmeg
½ t. ground cloves

Mix the butter and sugar, then the applesauce, egg, four cups of flour and baking soda. Mix the flavoring and fruits and nuts last. Flour all fruit well with one-half cup of flour before adding to the batter. Bake the mixture at 275 degrees for three to three and three-quarter hours (or until done when tested) in a paper-lined, greased pan. Also, have a pan of water on the bottom shelf of the oven while baking is in progress. Wine or bourbon may be poured onto the top of the cake when it is cooled. Put the cake in a covered, metal can and allow the cake to season. Actually, the cake can be baked in the metal can in which the cake may be covered and allowed to season. (These cakes have been known to prompt declarations of war when others eat more than their fair share.)

PEEDEE

Peedee Walker stood there, as he did practically every morning, in the dark and waiting to catch the bus into the city. This time, however, he carried a burlap bag stuffed with live Plymouth Rock chickens. He hoped to sell them for his mama at a farmers's market near the stockyards where he worked as a cattle feeder.

Several trucks and cars, obscured by the fog and misting rain, sped past Peedee. He waved at some of the trucks, thinking they might be the bus. None stopped.

The noise and wakes caused by passing vehicles made the chickens more nervous than they already were. Peedee grew nervous, too, and anxious. The bus was about a half-hour late. Peedee blamed the bus's delay on the war, an excuse nearly everyone now used for things that didn't go right.

Peedee had about decided he had missed the bus when he spotted it through the fog and rain a short distance away. He quickly dropped the bag and began frantically crisscrossing his arms above his head and jumping up and down. The bus's headlights reflected off the fish-belly-white underside of his raised arms. Much to his relief, the bus, which had begun to slow down about the time Peedee saw it, stopped a few feet beyond where he stood.

Peedee's heart raced as he hoisted the bag of chickens and ran toward the bus. The front door of the bus swung open. "Sorry I'm late, Peedee," the driver called out. "There's a war on, you know."

Peedee nodded.

"Did you think I'd really leave you?"

"Well, I knowed iffin you seen me you'd be a'stoppin'. But I watn't shore you could see me, what with all this here fog and all," Peedee said, lifting the bag as he stepped up into the bus.

"Truth is," the driver said, closing the door, "I didn't see you. I just figured you'd be where I usually pick you up. And you were."

"I thank you kindly," Peedee said as he set the bag down. He reached deep into the right pocket of his overalls for the bus fare, withdrew his hand, and dropped several coins into the driver's outstretched palm. "I'm sorry I ain't got the right 'mount this mornin'," he told the driver while studying the bus's interior and its sleeping passengers.

The driver gave Peedee his change. "Looks to me like you got a bus load," Peedee said, searching the muted, dim-lit interior for a seat.

"Yeah, and from the way they talk, I believe most of them are city folk from up north," the driver said. He nodded his head backward. "I think you can find a seat for you and your sack way toward the back."

Peedee put away his change, bent over, and, using both hands, picked up the bag of chickens. He stepped toward the rear of the bus just as it suddenly jerked forward. Peedee fell hard to the floor, pushing his cargo of chickens into the air as he did so.

The cord that secured the mouth of the bag broke as the bag slammed against an empty seat four rows down. Plymouth Rocks exploded in terror through the opening of their burlap prison. Several chickens flew cackling onto the laps of passengers or into their chests and faces. Other chickens, their red, single combs topping off their frenzied faces, raced wildly back and forth in panic down the aisle and under seats, seeking safety wherever they could find it.

All the while, passengers, many climbing over each other, rushed for the chicken-occupied aisle screaming, yelling, wailing, and cursing. They beat off spooked poultry with newspapers, magazines, pillows, purses, shoes, hats, and bare hands. One man, not content to fight them off with his hands and feet, swung a briefcase in the air, missing a chicken but catching another passenger squarely against the right side of his head.

Meanwhile, Peedee regained his footing. He picked up his bag and brushed aside with his other hand gray, barred feathers that now wafted about the inside of the bus. He tried to calm both the passengers and the chickens. "They ain't gonna hurt y'all none," he counseled the passengers. "They's just chickens. Here chickee, chickee, chickee," he called to the chickens. Neither passengers nor chickens paid Peedee any mind.

The only passengers untouched by the pandemonium sat on the bus's back row. They gaped at the spectacle to their front, not sure of what to do. They agreed, however, with Peedee. The chickens wouldn't hurt anybody. The back-row riders saw no need for the violence. Other than to grab two or three frightened fowl who chanced the rear area and to hand them over to a grateful Peedee, they did not join the tumult.

The driver, who battled chickens as he fought to maintain control over his vehicle, finally brought the bus to a stop and quickly opened the door. Passengers and chickens alike leaped out the door and into the fog.

After Peedee and the driver collected the few chickens that remained on the bus and returned them to the bag, the driver motioned to the passengers who stood outside that they could get back on board. But before he let them back on, the driver pointed to Peedee and then pointed to the door.

Peedee got off the bus. The passengers filed by Peedee as they returned to the blue and gray conveyance. "Redneck idiot," said one as he walked past Peedee. "Your mama and daddy must've been sister and brother."

"I'm sorry," Peedee muttered apologetically, "I didn't do hit on purpose."

The door to the bus closed. Peedee stood holding the bag with the luckless Plymouth Rocks that failed to take advantage of their opportunity to escape. He watched the bus disappear into the fog and then turned to look for more of his mama's chickens. He found and bagged as many as he could and began walking in the direction of the city miles away, hoping someone would stop and pick him up.

He spotted the bus coming back toward him. It passed him, slowed down, and turned around in a driveway a hundred or so yards away. The bus eased up beside Peedee and stopped. The door opened. Peedee, astonished, approached the opening and looked up at the driver. Peedee did not say anything. He heard singing and clapping coming from deep inside the bus. The driver slid out from under the steering wheel and stepped into the bus's stairwell.

"Peedee," the driver said, "come on, you can get back on. Seems like we've almost got ourselves another riot, right here on the bus. A fellow who calls himself a preacher come up from the back of the bus after I left you, complaining about me leaving you out there like I did. He said Jesus would've never done what I done to you and what happened wasn't your fault nohow."

"Well, hit mighta been my fault, but I didn't mean to do hit," Peedee assured the driver.

"The preacher, he said that, too—that you didn't let the chickens loose on purpose. Anyway, when I threatened to throw him off the bus, too, then all them in the back, they started singing and clapping and saying they weren't gonna stop until I come back and got you. The other passengers then started yelling and carrying on, wanting me to do something. So, I come on back for you so everybody could calm down and I could get on to the bus depot."

"Besides, you missed one," said a smiling passenger who appeared at the top of the stairwell with a chicken under his arm and talked with a northern accent. The passenger handed the gray bird down to the driver.

Peedee thanked the passenger and took the chicken from the driver. He dropped the chicken gently into the bag and, with the driver watching him closely and telling him to make sure it was good and tight, retied the cord around the bag's opening. As he got onto the bus, Peedee swung the bag over his left shoulder. The singing and clapping stopped when he reached the top step.

"I 'preciate you a'turnin' 'round and a'comin' back for me like you done. I shore hope hit don't make you late or nothin'. I wouldn't want you to git into no kinda trouble on 'counta me," Peedee told the driver as he looked for a place to sit and store his bag of chickens.

"This time, Peedee, I'll wait till you find yourself a seat before I start off. I sure don't want no more trouble out of them back yonder," the driver said, jerking his right thumb over his shoulder.

Peedee, tightly gripping the top of the bag with one hand and sliding his hand along the luggage rack with the other, inched carefully toward the smiling black faces at the end of the aisle straight ahead. He passed by the man who earlier had questioned his parentage. The man, whose face carried a mean expression, would not look at Peedee. He mumbled something, but Peedee could not quite understand him. It was something about the driver ought to throw some other idiots off the bus, too.

Peedee found a vacant seat on the left side of the bus immediately in front of his black saviors and their leader. He set his chickens on the seat's window side and sat down beside the bag. He turned to those behind him. "I'm Peedee Walker and I'm mucha obliged to all y'all for a'standin' up for me like y'all done. That there'd been a long walk," Peedee said.

"Why," said a tall, pencil-thin, elderly black man who cuddled a tattered Bible and wore a clerical collar, "don't you know the Bible, right there in *Galatians*, it say bear one 'nother's burdens. Somebody needed to help you with that big ol' sack."

"How far you a'goin'?" Peedee asked.

"Not too far now. Just to Cureton. I got grands there I ain't seen since the war be started. I'm goan be livin' with them a spell," said the black man. "Got to. My boy, he done be called up by Mr. Roosevelt."

Peedee opened the bag, reached in, and removed a young rooster. He handed it to the black man. "You take this here, why don't you? Y'all can make some chicken bog or somethin' other with hit."

The black man thanked Peedee and took the chicken. He held it in his lap atop his Bible and stroked its head until the bus made the next stop. The bus driver opened the bus's door and, looking into the rear view mirror above his head, announced, "Cureton. All out for Cureton."

The black preacher stood to leave. "Ain't goan let nobody kill this chicken," he said to Peedee. "No, sirree. Ain't nobody goan ring his neck or chop it off. I done give him a name. Can't kill no chicken what's got a name, you know. Wouldn't be right. Be like killin' a person."

"You really give hit a name?"

"Sho did. Named him Peedee."

Prue Goolsby's Recipe for Chicken Bog

2 pkg. chicken breasts (3 lbs.)
2 pkg. chicken thighs (2 lbs.)
1 green pepper
1 onion
1 stick margarine
2 lbs. long grain rice (don't use an instant rice)
½ lb. bacon
1 T. salt
1 T. pepper
1 12-oz. pkg. small breakfast sausage links
1 c. white wine

Cover the chicken and sausage in a large pot with enough water in the pot so that there will be six cups of broth left after the chicken and sausage are cooked. After bringing the water to a boil, turn the heat to low. Allow the chicken and sausage to cook for about an hour or until the chicken is tender.

Meanwhile, chop up the onion and bell pepper. Soak the rice in a bowl of cold water, making sure the rice is covered.

After the chicken and sausage are cooked, remove both from the pot and allow each to cool. Empty the pot, saving the broth. Strip the chicken from the bones, throwing away the skin and the bones. The strips should be a little larger than bite size.

Slowly cook the bacon in a pot until it is crisp. Remove the bacon from the pot, leaving the grease in the pot. Let the bacon drain. Put the chopped-up onion and green pepper into the pot and brown. Add six cups of broth and one cup of wine. Add the salt and pepper. Bring the mixture to a boil and add the chicken and sausage. After draining the rice, put it into the pot along with the stick of margarine. Stir the mixture well. Cover the pot and put the pot into the oven pre-heated to 350 degrees. Cook for an hour or so or until the rice is tender and there is no more liquid. (Do not stir the rice after it has been placed into the oven.)

Remove and serve it hot. Crumble the bacon on top of each serving of rice and serve the chicken bog with sweet potato biscuits and either cole slaw alone or cole slaw and barbecue if you truly want to pig out.

      Serves: A bunch (about ten people).

      Note: Try not to think of Peedee.

HONEY-MADE
SOFT DRINKS

Clarence Cowart, Dixie Water Bottling Company's production manager, stood with his diminutive subordinate behind the bottling room in the warehouse area of the plant surveying stacks of filled and unfilled bottles nestled in yellow wooden crates. "Shorty, how many cases of those things do we have left, you reckon?"

"I counted twenty cases awhile ago, fourteen grape and six orange," Shorty said. "Or was it fourteen orange and six grape. I don't remember exactly."

"Oh, it doesn't matter how many we got of each kind. Fact is we still have twenty cases of them, orange or grape. Dad gumit, I had hoped they'd all sell and we wouldn't have to fool with them."

"Do you want me to start pouring the bottles out?"

"Well, not right now I don't. I've got other things for you to do," Cowart replied as he opened the door to the bottling room.

An increased demand and a limited allotment had caused Dixie Water to run low on sugar during World War II's third summer. Cowart had decided to find a sugar substitute for the flavored drinks he bottled and to use the sugar for the colas. He had driven to Maryville and purchased a large quantity of honey. Returning to the plant, he had experimented using the honey as a sweetener. When he had satisfied himself that the taste of the orange and grape sodas approximated those made with sugar, especially after he added some other ingredients, he had bottled two hundred cases. Later, after he had received more sugar, the sugar-made drinks had been swapped for what remained of the honey-made ones.

Cowart stepped into the bottling room. Just as he pushed the button that activated the bottling machinery, he spotted a figure wearing a navy-blue suit and carrying a white Bible. "Hey, you can't be in here," Cowart yelled.

"The Lord-ah sent me-ah," the man replied.

"Mr. Lloyd? I don't know no Mr. Lloyd."

"No, sir. I said the Lord-ah sent me-ah. I-ah have come here-ah to buy-ah some drinks-ah," he announced, extending his right hand in Christian-fellowship and straining to be heard above the din of bottles being cleaned and filled by machine.

"To buy some drinks?" Cowart repeated. "You got a wholesaler's stamp?"

The man bent his head backwards and looked toward the ceiling, "The Lord-ah done told me-ah I don't need-ah no stamp-ah."

Cowart motioned the man out of the bottling room into the front office on the other side of the door. He followed the man through the doorway. "Look here, I can't help what the Lord done told you," Cowart said, closing the door behind him. "The governor says you've gotta have a wholesaler's stamp."

"I ain't-ah got no stamp-ah."

"What you need drinks for anyhow?" Cowart asked.

"Excuse me, sir-ah. Where are my manners-ah? I'm Brother T.J. LaGrange-ah and I'm conducting a revival-ah out on East Main-ah. It gets mighty hot-ah under the tent-ah and folks-ah do get thirsty-ah."

Cowart relaxed. Then he suddenly had a thought. "You know, I just might be able to help you after all."

"See there-ah. I knew the Lord-ah sent me to the right place-ah. I knew that-ah as soon as I saw you-ah. You-ah look like a man-ah what's been washed in the blood-ah."

"Any red stuff you see on me this morning ain't blood. It's strawberry syrup 'cause that's what we're bottling," Cowart laughed. "Look, we've got some orange and grape drinks out in the back. They're what you might call seconds. You know, they ain't perfect. They got a slight flaw in them."

"They got a what in them?" Brother LaGrange asked in a normal voice.

"Well, it ain't nothing in them. I mean, it ain't nothing you can see. I used honey instead of sugar to make them with after I run out of sugar. We picked them back up at the stores after we made drinks the way they're suppose to be made. We don't want to sell them since they ain't perfect and I just ain't got around to opening the bottles up and emptying the stuff out. You think you might want some of them? If so, we'll let you have them at a good price."

"How many you got?"

"Oh, I think about twenty cases, most of them grape . . . or orange. One or the other," Cowart answered.

"How much you want for them?" Brother LaGrange asked, squinting his eyes as he looked at Cowart and holding his Bible in both hands at chest level where Cowart was sure to see it.

"Since they're seconds," Cowart said, eyeing the Bible, "how about I let you have them for thirty cents a case, plus the deposit on the bottles and flats?"

"What about that there stamp you asked about?"

"You don't need one for seconds. Least, I don't think you do. I won't say anything if you won't."

"In that case," Brother LaGrange said, still disdaining his preacher voice, "I'll buy ten cases if you'll deliver them to my tent before four o'clock this afternoon. I'm going to be preaching about hellfire tonight and I expect people are gonna feel kinda hot as they think about them flames and all that sulfur down there."

"I'll get them there by four. Heck, we'll even ice them down for you," Cowart advised, pleased mightily with himself for having unloaded sodas that he had intended to pour out. "Just pay the fellow what brings them out to you. Now, don't forget these drinks are seconds. Folks what don't like them, they ain't gotta drink them. And there ain't no money-back guarantee what comes with them. You got that?"

"Yes, sir. I understand. And I'm much obliged to you for selling them to me. God'll bless you for what you done did." Brother LaGrange turned and walked out the front door onto the street. As he went, he whistled the chorus of "Drinking Water Drawn by Jesus" until he got to the words "I'll never, no never, thirst again." He sang these and then resumed his whistling.

That evening as he sat down to eat his supper of chicken and rice casserole, Cowart smiled at his wife across the table. "You know those grape and orange drinks I made with honey and had left over?" She nodded. "I sold ten cases of them to a tent preacher this morning."

The telephone interrupted their conversation. "I'll get it," Cowart said. He pushed back his chair. "It's probably for me anyhow."

He picked up the telephone, holding the receiver to his ear with one hand and the stand on which the mouthpiece was mounted with the other. "Hello."

"Mr. Cowart, this here's Shorty. I hate calling you at home. I tried to catch you before you left the plant but I musta missed you."

"Yeah, Shorty, what is it? I just sat down to eat my supper."

"Yes, sir. Anyways, after I took them drinks out there to the tent like you told me to, I opened me up one of them grapes. It tasted a little funny to me. I just thought you might want to know. It was kinda bubbling like, too."

"They're not supposed to taste like sugar-made grapes, Shorty. I told the man they were seconds. Anyhow, it's too late for me to do anything about it tonight. I'll see you in the morning." Cowart placed the receiver back onto the switchhook and returned to the supper table. His wife asked who had called. Cowart told her it was Shorty from the plant and what he had said.

"Aren't you worried about those drinks tasting funny?" she asked.

"No. Why should I be?" he responded.

"Because, if there is something wrong with them and somebody gets sick he'll sue the plant for violating the pure food law or something. And if that happens, you can kiss your job good-bye. That's why."

After a fitful night, Cowart arose the next morning, dressed, skipped breakfast and the family's morning devotional, and headed for the plant anxious to examine the honey-made softdrinks. In dawn's light, he made out a figure who stood at the front door of the plant. It was Brother LaGrange. Cowart guessed he was there to complain about the drinks.

"Mister," Brother LaGrange called out as Cowart approached, "I want to talk to you about them there drinks you sold me yesterday."

Cowart attempted to brush past him. "If you got anything to say about those drinks, you get in touch with our lawyer, Mr. Morris Snellgrove. Now, if you'll get out of my way and let me unlock the door, I gotta get to work."

"What do I want to talk to your lawyer for? I'm here to buy them other ten cases. You know, after we served them drinks at the meeting last night, why, people talked tongue like they never talked it before. They acted exactly like them mockers said the disciples acted on the day of Pentecost. They said the disciples acted like they was filled with new wine." Brother LaGrange opened his white Bible, turned to the second chapter of *Acts*, verse thirteen, and pointed his finger at the page. "Looka right here."

"I'll take your word for it," Cowart said. He unlocked the door, walked into the outer office, and closed the door behind him. Cowart left Brother LaGrange standing outside and wondering what was the matter.

Cowart ran to the rear of the plant, turned on the overhead lights, and went to the pallet that held the ten cases of honey-made softdrinks. He withdrew a bottle from a case, overlapped the crown on the edge of a nearby table, and brought his fist down hard onto the top of the bottle. The bottlecap popped off. The purple liquid inside burbled upward and overflowed the bottle. Cowart brought the mouth of the bottle to his own and took a sip. He swished it around and spit it out onto the floor. "I'll just be," he said. "The dang stuff's done fermented."

Prue Goolsby's Recipe for Chicken and Rice Casserole

1 can cream of chicken soup
1 can cream of mushroom soup
1 can cream of celery soup
½ stick butter, melted
1 ½ c. regular rice
1 ½ soup cans water
2 T. sherry or cooking sherry
6 pieces boned chicken breast
salt and pepper to taste

Mix all the ingredients except the chicken and salt and pepper. Pour the mixture into a large, deep casserole dish. Place the chicken pieces on top and sprinkle with the salt and pepper. Cover with a top or foil. Bake in a 325-degree oven for two hours or a 400-degree oven for one hour and fifteen minutes. Test the rice for doneness. If the rice is crunchy, then bake the chicken and rice mixture longer until done.

Serves: Four to six persons (since this recipe is so good, count on serving the minimum number; if it serves six, then two of the other four must be sick or something).

A GREEN FLY
IN ONE OF OUR
ORANGE DRINKS?

✤

Clarence Cowart sat opposite of Alfred Simons, the owner of Dixie Water Bottling Company. "A green fly?" Cowart said, his eyes opened wide. "Why, Mr. Simons, that just can't be. A green fly in one of our orange drinks?"

"Well, that's what the State man says, Clarence," Simons told his production manager. Simons sat behind a desk covered in trade magazines and bills. He held a newspaper whose headline announced the capture of Rome by Mark Clark's Fifth Army. "He says the fellow who runs Lester's Oyster Bar right outside of Cureton reported it to him. He also said the man's talking about suing us. Claims he drank some of it before he noticed the fly and it made him sick."

"Did he say what his name was?" Cowart asked, his voice marked by the concern he felt.

"No. He just said it was the man who runs Lester's Oyster Bar near Cureton."

"Well, if it's okay with you, if I get through bottling early this afternoon, I'll take the pickup and drive up there and see what this thing's all about. I can't understand how an orange drink with a green fly in it could pass through two inspections without somebody's catching it. I mean anybody could spot a green fly in an orange drink," Cowart said as he turned to walk from Simons's office and return to the bottling room. "It'd stick out like a hog at a barbecue."

"I sure hope you can find out something. Frankly, I'm more worried about the army and them not letting us sell them any more drinks than what the State might do to us, if it's true," Simons said.

Cowart left Simons's office and walked into the bottling room nearby. An almost deafening noise enveloped the room. Cowart stood for a moment, watching the soaker disgorge clean, empty bottles that twisted and whirled down a lathered conveyor belt to be inspected, filled with syrup and carbonated water, crowned with a bottle cap, inspected again, labeled, and cased. How was it possible, he kept asking himself, for a green fly to get into one of his drinks, one of his orange drinks at that, and not be detected?

That afternoon, after the bottling room had been washed down and the broken glass and other debris swept up, Cowart turned off the lights and walked out. He got into the plant's pickup truck, drove it to the rear of the building, and pulled up beside the gasoline pump. He got out and moved the pump handle back and forth until a scarlet fluid partially filled the glass globe. He removed the gas cap to the pickup and placed the nozzle of the gasoline pump into the intake pipe of the gas tank. Prince Albert Mason, the plant's soaker operator, stood nearby. "What you still doing here, Prince?"

Prince, whose left leg polio had deformed, hobbled over to the gas pump. "I'm waiting on Shorty. He had to run down to the Green Front. He's gonna take me home." Prince leaned against the body of the pickup, bracing himself. "You know one thing, Mr. Cowart, I've been studying about that there fly. You say it was a green fly, ain't that right?"

"I ain't seen it. But that's what the State man told Mr. Simons. What about it? A fly is a fly as far as I'm concerned."

"Why, Mr. Cowart, a green fly, he hangs 'round privies. We ain't got no privies 'round here. We got commodes. Two things a privy's got a commode ain't got and that's green flies and chickens."

Cowart grinned. "Is what you're trying to say, Prince, is we'd better be on the look out also for a bottle with a chicken in it?" He removed the nozzle from the truck and hooked it onto the pump. He screwed on the gas cap and opened the door to the cab.

"No, sir," Prince said, laughing. "Though that'd be something to see, sure 'nough. I mean a chicken in an orange drink. That'd sure be funny, wouldn't it, Mr. Cowart."

"What's your point, Prince? I gotta get on up to Cureton."

"Well, it's this. That fly, he come from a privy or something dead. He ain't come from no bottling plant."

"Prince, did it ever occur to you that the fly could've been in the bottle when it got to the plant and that the bottle went through the soaker and all without being flushed out, without anybody seeing it?" Cowart got into the truck and cranked its motor. He leaned out the window. "I'll see you in the morning. You and Shorty, don't y'all drink too much of that wine tonight, you hear?"

"You know I don't drink, Mr. Cowart. Shorty, he's getting it for his stomach. He say his preacher told him to do that. Somebody the preacher knows—a fellow named Paul—told him wine's real good for your stomach."

"Well, you tell Shorty not to treat his stomach too much with it or he'll be without a job if he ain't here for work tomorrow morning."

"Yes, sir. See you, Mr. Cowart," Prince called as Cowart drove into the alley leading to the street.

The trip to Cureton seemed to take forever. Cowart stopped at the traffic light in downtown Cureton. He looked around to see if there was anyone close by from whom he could obtain directions to Lester's Oyster Bar. Seeing no one, he drove to a service station across from the town square. A grossly overweight attendant eating a piece of cornbread on which he had poured sugar cane syrup ambled from the station up to the truck. He craned his head to read the sign on the truck's driver-side door.

"Well, now," he said, his mouth full and his lips covered with syrup, "if it ain't somebody what works with the company what's done gone to puttin' green flies in its big old orange drinks. I guess y'all start puttin' red worms in your strawberries next," the attendant jeered. "And then y'all'll put yellow jackets in the root beers; spice 'em up a little bit, know what I mean? Y'all don't charge nothin' extra for them flies, do you?"

"Well, I see you been talking to the man at Lester's Oyster Bar," Cowart said, passing off the insults.

"Yeah. Dewey Lester. He's been 'round here braggin' 'bout how he was gonna get rich and all 'cause he found that there fly in y'all's orange drink. Old Dewey, he said he was gonna sue y'all for all y'all're worth."

"Is that right? Can you tell me where I can find his place?"

"It ain't hard to find. Just stay on Oil Mill Road. It's 'bout a mile or so out of town on the left there. You'll see a brand new sign side the road with'n his name on it. I believe y'all the one what give him the sign. Just shows you can't help out nobody these days, don't it?"

"Much obliged," Cowart said. He put the truck in first gear and pulled past the attendant. A fat hand covered in cornbread crumbs and syrup waved a goodbye to Cowart who did not wave back. He drove onto the street, turned right, and headed for Oil Mill Road.

When he saw the Lester's Oyster Bar sign, he slowed down, turned, and crossed over the concrete culvert that spanned a ditch out in front of the establishment. A mule and wagon stood in a vacant area to the right of the building, an abandoned garage. The structure's tin roof had long since rusted to a dark brown. Its siding of tar paper flapped where strong winds and vandals had torn it, exposing wood turned gray beneath. The building sat almost flush with the ground. A screen door, ripped and punctured all over but still advertising its sponsor, opened onto the front parking lot and screened out little, if anything. Rusted signs plastered the front of the building in stark contrast to the new sign beside the road.

Cowart parked next to the mule and wagon and got out of the pickup. The area was the only dry place to park. A recent rain had covered the front parking lot with water. He walked around to the front, stepped on tiptoes as he walked through the water, and opened the screen door. Surface water had seeped inside and had flooded most of the oyster bar's floor close to the door.

As he sloshed inside and stepped up onto a low, wooden platform that supported the oyster bar's counter and other fixtures, Cowart saw a middle-age man seated on a bar stool at a counter that stretched across the entire back of the bar. The man was eating a hotdog. Behind the counter stood a kerosene stove and a corroded metal sink that once held iced-down oysters. Slow flames on one of the stove's burners heated a metal pot that contained several frankfurters and water. Another burner kept a pot of chili warm. Flies, green and black ones, surrounded the man and his hotdog, the sink, and the stove.

"Are you the owner?" Cowart asked as he stepped up to the bar.

The man turned toward Cowart, one hand holding the hotdog and the other a soft drink. His jaws worked sideways as he chewed away at the hotdog. When he swallowed, his Adam's apple danced, his head bobbed, and his eyes bulged outward.

"Naw, he ain't the owner. I am. Who wants to know?" The gruff voice came from behind the counter to the left of the man eating the hotdog.

Cowart looked over the counter in the direction of the voice. He was stunned to see a man who was squatted over a hole in the floor with his britches pulled down to just above his ankles. "Iffin you a'lookin' for oysters, mister, I ain't got nar'un. It's July, you know. I can fix you a hotdog, though. Say, Rayford, hand me some of them there napkins, iffin you don't mind."

The man at the counter put down his hotdog to the delight of the flies and reached for the stack of napkins to his right. He grabbed a handful and then leaned over the counter and held them out to the owner's outstretched hand.

"Thank you kindly, Rayford," he said. "Hey, mister, you from Dixie Water, ain't you?" he said, noticing

Cowart's uniform as Cowart drew closer to the counter. "What you a'doin' up this here way?" He used the napkins.

"I'm here about that fly business," Cowart said, turning away.

The owner raised his trousers to his hips, buttoned his fly, and buckled his belt. He reset two planks over the hole. A squadron of green flies hit the area after he moved away. He came to the counter. "Dixie Water Bottlin' Company," he hummed, "makers of Dixie Water, 'the drink with mornin' freshness,' so they say. What they don't say is they also make orange drinks that'll give you mornin' sickness 'cause they put green flies in them."

"We don't say it, 'cause it ain't true," Cowart asserted in a calm voice.

"It ain't, huh? You couldn't prove it none by me."

"You mind if I see the bottle you claim's got a fly in it?" Cowart asked.

The owner ignored Cowart. "You want 'nother hotdog, Rayford?"

"Huh-uh, I done ate four already. I'm 'bout full up." Rayford washed down what remained of his hotdog with his soft drink, his jaws still working sideways. "I'll take 'nother one of them there orange sodas, though."

Lester opened Rayford a bottle of orange drink, one made by a Dixie Water competitor, and handed it to him across the counter. Rayford picked the bottle up, took a swallow, and put the bottle down. A green fly immediately pounced on the lip of bottle and skittered around its rim as Rayford grasped the waist of the bottle.

When he saw this, Cowart pointed to the bottle. "Mr. Lester, that's how that fly got into your drink, I believe."

"Say what?" Lester leaned against the counter and looked down at Rayford's orange. The fly flew away when Lester's body caused the counter to give somewhat and to shake the bottle. "I don't see nothin'. What you a'talkin' about anyways?"

"There was a fly on the mouth of that bottle, but he flew off when you bumped against the counter and made the bottle sway," Cowart explained. "That's probably what happened to your orange. A fly got on the mouth of the bottle and probably fell in or flew in, one. Heck, there's flies everywhere in here," he said, fanning flies away with the back of right hand. "I don't understand why the health department hadn't closed you up. The place is filthy. The cleanest things you got in here are the soft drinks and that's only because they got caps on them," Cowart said looking all around. "Where is your health certificate anyhow? Everybody knows it's against the law for somebody to sell food and not have a health certificate."

Lester looked surprised at the question. "Why, I don't sell nothin' but oysters and only when they's in season, you know, durin' 'r' months. This here ain't no 'r' month. You don't need no health certificate if you ain't got no oysters. Them hotdogs, they don't count. I just sell them for fun. You don't think I'm supposed to have me no health certificate, do you Rayford?"

"Well now," Rayford mused, rubbing his stubbed chin, "I was just sittin' here a'thinkin'. Roosevelt said we had to have stamps and things for some stuff. You know, stamps for shoes. Stickers for gas. 'Course, I don't need no gas sticker. I ain't got no car or nothin'. All I got is my mule. 'Course now, he's got gas, but he don't drink it to get it," Rayford said. He chuckled at his attempt to be funny. No one else chuckled or even smiled.

"Rayford, I ain't a'talkin' about no ration stamps and stickers. I'm a'talkin' about health certificates. Roosevelt ain't got nothin' to do with no health certificates." Lester waved away some flies. He reached behind and above his own head and pulled down from a top shelf an opened orange drink with a green fly that floated on top of the reddish-yellow liquid in the bottle. "You say you want to see my bottle? If you want to see somethin' that'll just plum make you sick to look at it, you just look at this here? Look here what y'all done. Y'all tried to poison me, ain't you?"

"That drink's been opened," Cowart remarked on seeing the bottle and its green guest for the first time

"Of course it's been opened. I took a couple of swallows 'fore I seen that there fly was in it. I still get the dry heaves when I think about it. You ever see anything what looks nastier than this here orange?"

"I sure have. I'm standing in it." Cowart looked at Rayford who had not moved from the counter. "Your name's Rayford?"

"Yes, sir. Rayford Junior Harper. Please to meet you. What be your name?" Rayford stuck out his hand. Cowart refused to take it. Rayford pulled his hand back, but not before he batted at a fly or two to cover the awkwardness of an extended hand not shaken in greeting.

"Do you spell 'Rayford' with a 'y'?" Cowart asked.
"What's a 'y'?"

"Never mind," Cowart said. He withdrew a small pad and pencil from his shirt pocket, turned a couple of pages, and wrote down Rayford's name using a "y." "How in the world can you eat those hotdogs, Rayford? I mean, look at this place. It's got more flies than any two-seater outhouse I ever seen."

"Well," he said, "I was hungry, I reckon. And besides, he makes the best hotdog chili there is."

Cowart turned to wade back out the front door. "Lester, since you've seen fit to put the State man on us, I'm gonna return you the favor. As soon as I get back to the plant, I'm calling the health department. They'll probably put you in jail for selling food without a food permit. And I hope they do."

Lester called after Cowart. "Hey, mister. Mister, wait a minute. No hard feelin's. Look here, why don't you, I'll get in touch with the State man and I'll tell him it was all a big mistake 'bout the fly. Look at what I'm a'doin'. I'm a'pourin' the orange drink out right now." Lester turned the bottle upside down in the sink. The green fly rode the orange fluid out of the bottle and down the drain.

"Mister, hey mister, it's all gone. Here, have a hotdog. It's for free. I'll even put some of my chili on it for you. I got onions, too, if you want them." Lester held out a hotdog to Cowart who stopped momentarily at the door and looked back. A formation of flies dove for the hotdog.

"No, thanks. Give it to Rayford." Cowart snapped as he opened the door and walked out.

"Thank you kindly, mister," Rayford yelled to Cowart, snatching the hotdog from Lester's hand and the fly group that buzzed near it. "I'll take it home and give it to my maw. She loves hotdogs 'cause they ain't hard on her gums. And the hotdogs in here, they's good ones, too. Real good ones. She'll really 'preciate it."

"You ain't a'goin' nowheres with my hotdog unless you pay me ten cents for it," Lester told him.

As the screen door shut, Cowart turned and saw Rayford stand up and reach deep into his right pocket with his left hand. His right hand clutched the hotdog around which more flies swarmed as he struggled to get the change he needed. Rayford pulled out two nickels and gave them to Lester and then blew at the flies on his hotdog. "Shoo," he said. "Shoo."

Cowart got into his truck and pressed down on the starter with his foot. He let the motor run for a moment before putting the gear into reverse, backing up, and driving forward out onto the highway. As he drove toward the plant, he found himself thinking of verse seventeen of the eighteenth chapter of *Proverbs*, a verse he and his family had discussed at the breakfast table the day before during their morning devotional. *How did it go exactly?* he asked himself. He couldn't recall. He had no trouble, however, remembering the meaning of the verse: a man's story seems right, until you look into it.

Prue Goolsby's Recipe for Hotdog Chili (No Green Flies)

1 lb. ground beef
1 t. granulated onion
1 heaping t. chili powder
½ t. red pepper
1 t. black pepper
½ t. salt
½ t. Worcestershire sauce water to cover

Place all the ingredients in a pan. Stir well to crumble the beef. Boil until the meat is done; however, keep the meat covered with water and warm while preparing the hotdogs. Drain the liquid from the meat as the meat is taken directly from the pot and spread onto the hotdog.

Serves: Covers about eight to ten hotdogs (counting what spills off into your lap when you overload the hotdog).

Note: For the best hotdog on the planet, use mild Italian sausages instead of wieners and saute the onions (preferably Vidalia) rather than serve them raw. If you prefer raw onions, try putting cole slaw on the hotdogs in addition to the onions and chili.

THE CURSE ON
THE RAILROAD MAN

After a supper of country-fried steak, gravy, and mashed potatoes, my father and I adjourned to our favorite rocking chairs on the front porch. "What do you mean you put a curse on a railroad man one time?" I asked him. "That doesn't sound to me like a very Christian thing to do. How'd you come to do that?"

"Oh, it's Christian all right," my father said. "Your mama's part to blame for me doing it, though."

"Mama?"

"Yeah, your mama. I'd interviewed for a job with the railroad. The man what was doing the hiring, he told me to come back Monday morning and he'd let me know if I had the job or not. It was a good job and one I really wanted. Shoot, I could just see myself, hanging on the side of a box car and motioning the engineer to back the train up. Or, riding in the caboose and leaning out the window and waving at folks along the tracks. I sure did want that job."

Dad stopped a moment, shook his head once sideways, and sighed. "The afternoon before I was to go back to see the railroad man I asked your mama to marry me. She told me she wouldn't do it unless I first joined the Methodist Church."

"You didn't belong to a church?" I inquired.

"Yeah. No. Well, I reckon you could call it 'belonging to a church.' I'd been going to the 'Barn Again Chapel,' least that's what me and my brothers called it. It wasn't no real church, if you know what I mean. This man, Wilbur Hood, he'd started holding church services a mile or so down the road from our house in an old abandoned barn. See, that's why we called it the Barn Again Chapel. Mama, she made us go there. It was just kinda hard, though, to worship Jesus in a barn."

"I thought Jesus was born in a barn," I said.

"Well, he was," he acknowledged, "but show me in the Bible where it says he preached in a barn."

"What about the curse on the railroad man?"

Dad crossed his legs, took a Lucky Strike out of his shirt pocket and tapped it a couple of times on the back of a Zippo lighter. He lit his cigarette and inhaled. "After I asked your mama to marry me and she told me what she wanted me to do first," he said, exhaling gray smoke, "I asked her when I had to do it. She told me I had to do it that night."

He drew more smoke into his lungs and let it seep out through his nostrils. "Now, I didn't object to joining the Methodist Church. I knew my mama wouldn't care. She just wanted me to go to church someplace or another. As I said, I didn't like going to the Barn Again Chapel anyway. It didn't even seem like church. We'd sit on drink crates, old milk cans, anything we could find, if we sit down at all. We didn't have no choir. No musical instruments, except when Uncle Cody'd come and bring his jaw's harp. I was ashamed to tell people I even went there. Like me, Brother Hood, didn't have no education or not much of one. He just up and started preaching one day. Claimed he had a vision one night after he'd been to a cock fight."

"What about the curse?" I asked again.

"I'm coming to that. Hand me that ash tray over there. This one's full."

I handed him another ash tray. He set it down by the full one.

"Your mama knew I didn't like going to the Barn Again Chapel. After I told her I'd join the Methodist Church like she wanted me to, she walked around the rest of the day like she'd saved some lost soul for Jesus. I think it meant more to her that I was joining the Methodist Church than me asking her to marry me. Matter of fact, it'd crossed by mind she might be tricking me into joining just so she could brag about it to the preacher or her Sunday School teacher.

"That night, the preacher, he preached on Jesus' putting a curse on a fig tree. Do you know the story?"

I told him I didn't.

"Well," he began, "one morning Jesus was on his way into town and he was hungry. He saw this fig tree there by the side of the road. He went over to it and didn't find no figs on it. This made him so mad. Now, can you picture Jesus getting mad about anything, especially a fig tree? Anyhow, Jesus got mad at this fig tree and he put a curse on it. The Bible says he told it, 'May you have no more figs ever again.' This fig tree, it just withered up. Right then and there.

"That's what Brother Orange talked on the night I joined the Methodist Church, Jesus' putting a curse on you. I thought, Lord have mercy, if Jesus can do that to a fig tree, just think what he could do to me if I didn't do what he wanted. Brother Orange got me all scared. I didn't know Jesus was like that, you know. He said people what smoked, and I smoked then just like I smoke now, was just exactly like that fig tree. He said people what drank was also just like that tree. I drank some in them days, too. Your mama didn't know I drank, though. But I knew Jesus knew. God and Jesus, they always know everything."

"Like Santa Claus," I said.

"Yeah, but Santa Claus ain't real. God and Jesus, they're real. Anyhow, I felt like Brother Orange also knew I drank 'cause he seemed to look right at me when he started talking about drinking. He said one day Jesus was gonna come up to each one of us and he was gonna make a personal inspection, just like he come up to and inspected that fig tree. And if we weren't bearing fruit or ready to help him or somebody else, he was gonna curse us and we were gonna wither up and we were gonna die. Yes, sir, he said we were gonna die. Heck, I wasn't but nineteen years old. I didn't want that happening to me. I wanted to get married and work for the railroad.

"I tell you, when Brother Orange gave the altar call, I didn't need your mama to nudge me down front. I went running down that aisle. I didn't even wait for the choir to start singing. I didn't want to end up like that fig tree. I didn't want Jesus' putting no curse on me. I was gonna join the Methodist Church. I was gonna quit smoking and I was gonna quit drinking. I was gonna be a changed man.

"So, I became a Methodist. Every time I eat figs I think about that night."

"I notice you still smoke and you'll still take a drink," I said, laughing.

"Anyhow," he said, ignoring my observation, "I went by the railroad office the next morning. I went in and asked for the man I'd been talking to, a man named Bauknight. After awhile he come in and told me to come on back to his office. I went on back. He told me I could have the job on one condition. I asked him what that was and he said I had to join his church. I asked him if it was a Methodist and he said no. I told him I couldn't join no other church, least not right then anyway 'cause I'd just joined the Methodist Church the night before.

"His face, it turned red, then it turned purple. He told me there were two kind of people he didn't like. He didn't like folks who pulled for Alabama and he didn't like Methodists. He said you're a Methodist and I bet you pull for Alabama, too. Up till then I really didn't care whether Alabama won or lost. I could care less. But from that day on, I've pulled for Alabama. Anyway, he told me I couldn't have the job.

"So when I joined the Methodist Church it cost me a job with the railroad. Just think, I could've been retired on a good railroad pension. Instead, I gotta live on the little bit of social security what Roosevelt give me."

"Did you say anything to Mr. Bauknight about him not hiring you because you were a Methodist?"

"I sure did. I told him about Jesus and the fig tree. Just like Brother Orange said, I told him Jesus was gonna come make a personal inspection of him one of these days."

"What'd he say to that?"

"He said good. He looked forward to it. Then he told me to get my sorry, no-good Methodist butt out of his office. That's when I put the curse on him, just like Jesus put on that fig tree. I said to him, 'Bauknight, may you have no children.' I figured the world'd be better off without any more the likes of him."

"Do you reckon your curse worked?" I asked.

"I can't say. But ain't none of them young'uns his wife give him got red hair and light skin like he's got. What do you think?"

Prue Goolsby's Recipe for Country-Fried Steak

6 pieces jiffy steak
1 ½ to 2 cups plain flour
1 ½ t. salt
½ t. pepper
2 large onions
3 T. salad oil

Put the flour, salt, and pepper into a large plastic bag and shake until they are mixed well. Add the steak and shake it until it is well coated with the flour mixture. Heat the oil in a large frying pan and fry the steak a few pieces at a time until the pieces are well browned and crusty on both sides, being careful not to burn or let the crust stick to the pan. If necessary, add more oil to the pan. Remove the steak and place it on a platter as it gets done. When all pieces have been fried, peel and slice the onions into about one-eighth-inch-thick slices and saute the slices in the drippings left in the pan. When the onions are just beginning to brown, remove them to a dish.

Make a gravy, using the drippings in the pan. Add one-fourth cup of flour mixed with two cups of water, one tablespoon of Kitchen Bouquet, one and one-half teaspoons Worcestershire Sauce, and salt and pepper to taste. Stir well. When the gravy begins to boil, turn the heat down to low and add the cooked steak and onions. Cover and cook for about fifteen minutes.

Serves: Four to six persons (most likely, four because it is so good it'll make you fight your grandma or the preacher's wife).

ALTAR CALL

T he Reverend June Leadlove's first impulse was to ignore the news article. So what if the newspaper complained about his Jaguar, his gold encircled fingers, his tailored suits, his several-thousand-square-foot home, and his European vacations. So what if his recent divorce resulted in his ex-wife's getting no alimony and no marital property.

If the paper's intent had been to persuade people not to attend the Blood of the Lamb Tabernacle, the opposite result, from all appearances, had occurred. For the first time since the tabernacle's dedication, an overflow crowd flocked into the sanctuary as ushers and other church workers finished the placement in the aisles of folding chairs borrowed from Sunday school rooms. The swell of humanity in the sanctuary gave it the look of an Easter Sunday. The newspaper story had brought them in, by the carload. People wanted to hear what Brother Leadlove had to say about the newspaper's allegations.

Brother Leadlove joined the song leader, choir, and congregation in singing the third verse of "Jesus Is Holding on Line One." The beat of tambourines against the combined sounds of organ and piano on a fast-paced tune like that always energized the worshipers. They next sang "Two Men in the River." On the second verse the song leader, Brother Berry Elmwood, joined the instrumentation with his trombone, a move that never failed to delight folks at the tabernacle. Everybody loved to hear Brother Elmwood play his trombone. They remembered the night he came to hear Brother Leadlove and got saved. They remembered how they cried when he told them about his drug addiction and his playing with bands in Memphis and New Orleans. They pointed to Brother Elmwood as proof that Jesus could indeed rescue the perishing.

When Brother Leadlove figured everyone had sung about all they cared to sing, he took the pulpit and the congregation became very still. He felt every eye. He sensed their concern. He knew they had questions. Too bad. He wasn't about to answer them. Well, he might answer one or two. He had drafted a sermon about ingratitude, a topic he felt would loosen purse strings. It always did. But it would have to wait, he concluded as he scanned the sanctuary.

"My friends," he began confidently, "y'all know what? Like James Brown, I feel good. I feel real good. For me to feel any better, I'd have to be in a boat on Lake Murray fishing with Jesus."

"Amen!" scores echoed joyfully, some jumping from their seats and clapping their hands.

"Yes, sir, I'd have to be fishing with the Savior to feel any better." He turned to his song leader. "Fishing with the Savior. Brother Elmwood, you ought to write a song and call it 'Fishing With the Savior.' That'd be a good one."

The congregation burst into applause, many shouting their approval.

Brother Leadlove grew more serious. "I thank y'all for coming here this morning. And to show my personal appreciation for y'all being here, I'm not gonna ask the ushers to take up a collection today. No, siree. So, you ushers back there, y'all just go on and have a seat. Put the plates away. All y'all can just close your purses and put your wallets back in your britches. If some of you women or little girls out there got some change knotted up in some old handkerchief like my mama used to do hers, well, just re-knot it. Reknot your hanky. There ain't gonna be no collection today. If the church runs into a problem 'cause we didn't take up a collection this morning, then I'll take care of it. I should be able to do that 'cause the paper says I'm rich and you know you can believe everything you read in the paper." He paused. "That is, if you're an idiot and I don't believe none of you are."

Again the amens came. They accompanied sounds of purses snapping shut and people moving in their seats. Brother Leadlove waited until things quieted down before he spoke again.

"You know, Jesus went home one time. Everybody there started talking about him, saying all kinds of bad things. Some folks asked, 'How'd he get so high and mighty all of a sudden? Who does he think he is, anyways?' Or, they'd say, 'I remember him when he was a boy down there working at his daddy's place, sawing wood and all.' They'd laugh and giggle at him and make fun of him. But you know what Jesus did? He tried to overlook what they were saying about him. He told them, 'A prophet is not without honor except in his own hometown.' Yes, sir, people everywhere else appreciated Jesus but not those folks where he grew up at. You know what they did, his own people? They weren't satisfied talking about him, putting the bad mouth on him. No, they ran him out of town. Not only that, they took him up on top of this hill. They took him up there, intending to throw him off of it. But you know what? Jesus, he didn't let them. He just simply broke loose from them and walked off. He went away from them, leaving them there with their mouths hanging wide open."

"Praise Jesus!" someone cried about twelve rows back. "Thank you, Jesus!" hollered another.

A tambourine player slapped her tambourine and shook it. "Yes, Jesus!" she screamed. The organist pressed down on the keyboard. The sanctuary reverberated with shouts of praise and thanksgiving.

He loosened his tie and unbuttoned the top button on his shirt. He threw his coat to Brother Elmwood, who draped it over his trombone stand. He ran a heavily ringed finger through the black, wavy strands of his toupee. "Do y'all want to join the paper in throwing me off a hilltop? Do y'all want me to walk off, to go away?"

The congregation erupted again amid angry shouts of no and pleas for him to stay.

"Jesus," he said, "had a bad reputation. Did you know that? Well, he did. Jesus had a bad reputation. They said he hung around with sinners, the wrong kind of folks. They said he hung around with drunkards. And with gluttons, they said. They said he hung around with, now get this, tax collectors. Today, we'd call them the IRS. How many of y'all like the IRS? Now, if folks would say stuff like that about Jesus, imagine what they'd say about his disciples. Look at what folks'll say today about his preachers?"

He reached down to the shelf beneath the pulpit and brought up a glass pitcher filled with water and a paper cup. He poured himself a cupful and drank it without pausing. "Now, you newspaper reporters out there, and I know you're out there, what you just saw me drink was not what y'all drink all the time. That wasn't no white liquor or gin. That was pure and tee water. Don't y'all go putting in the paper y'all saw me drinking liquor in the pulpit. It was just water, honest."

Laughter and praise Jesuses filled the sanctuary.

"What did that reporter write about me? She said, and I'm quoting her now, 'The Reverend Mr. Leadlove, according to sources, earns more in one year than most college presidents. He does this,' she said, and I'm quoting again, 'by preaching about Jesus and St. Paul, two persons who never made the big bucks, never owned a means of transportation, and never lived in a mansion.'"

In an angry voice, he yelled, "How would she know? Whoever heard of a reporter going to church anyway, unless it was to try and hurt somebody. Y'all know any reporter who goes to church? Do you? If you do, raise your hand." He tarried a moment and then surveyed the congregation. Seeing no hands raised, he said, "I thought so."

He removed the microphone from its stand and began walking slowly back and forth on the chancel. "No, Jesus didn't earn no big salary. He didn't earn no big bucks, to use their words. As long as they're drawing comparisons, I think it's fair for me to draw some, too. Ain't that fair?

So, I'm gonna draw me some comparisons. I've been preaching for twenty-eight years. I'm fifty-two years old. Until recently, I had a wife to support. I ain't in jail. I'm not under indictment for anything, least that I know of."

The congregation laughed again, but not as loud as before, which disappointed Brother Leadlove. He waited until the laughter subsided.

"Now follow me on this. How old was Jesus when he died? Thirty-three. How long did his ministry last? Three years. I wonder what Jesus would've gotten, what he would've owned, had he kept on preaching, teaching, healing, and casting out demons, and hadn't been crucified until he'd reach my age? I'll tell you one thing, people would've been giving him things other than precious oil for his feet. They'd been loaning him things other than donkeys to ride on or upper rooms to meet in. You know, the tomb he was buried in was one somebody let him borrow for three days.

"And old Paul, well he was a jailbird awaiting trial much of the time. But I'll tell you this, with all the traveling Paul done and the fix he was in somebody had to have helped him along. Had to have. Did Paul have a wife like I did one time? Let me ask you this, how come they don't never say nothing about the Pope? I mean, Lordy mercy, look at where he lives. Look how he travels. You talk about vacations, he's been all over the whole world. And he's going again, I hear. He's even been to South Carolina. Do you ever read about his house, his car? He's even got a special car, a 'Pope Mobile,' they call it. Maybe I ought to get me a special car with a bubble top and call it a 'Leadlove Limo.'" The crowd laughed. "No, y'all don't read about the Pope and all his church gives him. But y'all can read about poor old Brother Leadlove."

He took another swig of water. "Boy howdy, that's good stuff," he joked, hitting his chest with his fist. "And, of course, they had to write about my marital problems. You'd think some things would be private. But no, they had to tell the world, like it's anybody's business. They said my wife didn't get nothing when we got divorced. Why didn't she get anything? Why didn't the judge who heard our case give her any alimony or property? You want to know why she didn't get no alimony? Okay, I'll tell you. It grieves me to do so. It was because she committed adultery, that's why. The paper didn't print that, did it? Why didn't she get no property? Because I didn't get none either. That house they talk about, it didn't belong to me. It belonged to the church. If the Presbyterians can put their preacher in a manse, how come y'all can't put your preacher in a mansion?"

The congregation was on its feet. "Hallelujah! Hallelujah!" the flock yelled.

For thirty or forty more minutes he continued to defend himself. He drew an analogy between himself and King David's problem with his son Absalom. Finally, he fast forwarded to more modern times and spoke of Martin Luther's difficulties and how they mirrored his own. Nearly exhausted, he placed the microphone back on its stand, dropped his arms, took a step backward, brought himself to attention, and lifted his face toward heaven. "After Martin Luther nailed his theses to that door, you know what he said?" he asked softly, while his eyes focused skyward. "He said, 'Here I stand. I cannot do otherwise. God help me. Amen.'"

Brother Leadlove repeated several more times the words Luther addressed to the Diet of Worms. He paused, pulled his handkerchief from his coat pocket, and wiped his eyes. "Look at me now," he resumed. "Like Martin Luther four hundred years ago, here I stand. I cannot do otherwise. God help me. Amen."

He bowed his head and leaned into the pulpit. He picked up his Bible and held it aloft with his right hand. He looked out over the now quiet assembly. "Here I stand. Will you stand with me?" he asked quietly. "Will you stand with me?" he repeated. "And with Jesus?" he added. "Will you?" He nodded to Brother Elmwood.

Brother Elmwood stood, signaling the organist and pianist. They began softly playing "It's So Beautiful Over There," an invitational hymn Brother Elmwood wrote shortly after he got saved. As they played, Brother Leadlove kept pleading, "Will you stand with me and Jesus?" After the hymn played through twice, he assumed the position of a cross, his legs together, and his arms outspread. "Won't you stand with me and Jesus?" he pleaded. "Please, won't you do so right now, right where you are?" he whispered into the microphone.

People hesitated at first. Then, a few stood and a few more and a few more. As the minutes passed and more people stood, he said tearfully, "Thank you, Jesus."

The choir began to sing. He invited those standing to join him down front as a demonstration of their faith in him and in Jesus.

The first wave hit the aisles. When the choir began singing the invitational hymn's second verse, Brother Leadlove saw a stunning, beautiful figure ease into the aisle and join the next wave. Unlike the others, she was not crying or emotional. She did not look down or up. She looked straight at him as she walked forward.

Brother Elmwood, however, reached her first and hugged and kissed her on the cheek, leaving a wet spot where his lips had been. A woman whose profile duplicated Benjamin Franklin's and who had met almost every altar call Brother Leadlove had ever given prevented Brother Leadlove from reaching the pretty face with the dry eyes first.

"Bless you, sister," Brother Leadlove said, dismissing the altar-call veteran and heading quickly for the gorgeous creature who carried Brother Elmwood's mark on her cheek. He felt sweat pop out beneath his toupee and sensed his face glow red. "God bless you, sweet lady," he said to her.

Instead of merely hugging her and kissing her cheek, as Brother Elmwood had done, he put his right hand to the back of her head and brought her face up to his own. Brother Leadlove looked into her eyes. She did not pull back. He kissed her. She still did not pull back. He kissed her again. This time, he felt her tongue inside his mouth, moving between his upper lip and his gum line. "Jesus," he said when they separated. He retreated for a step or two, gasping for air.

Thankfully, he found a child standing nearby. He placed his hand on the child's head, steadied himself, and blessed him. Brother Leadlove kept his hand on the child until the dizziness subsided and he was certain he could move on.

Before Brother Leadlove turned to greet and bless others who came forward that morning, he went back to the woman whose kiss had caused him nearly to faint. Whispering, he instructed her to ask Brother Elmwood to bring her to his office after church. She gave a slight nod.

Brother Leadlove broke away when he could and went straight to his office. He remained for a moment at the door. He patted his toupee and smoothed down the hair on both sides of his head. He drew a deep breath and pushed the door open. Immediately upon seeing her, he lost his breath and felt himself go weak again. He feared he might pass out. He recovered and walked up to her. He thought about greeting her again with a holy kiss but lost his courage before he could execute the thought. Instead, he held out his hand. "I'm Brother Leadlove," he said.

"And I'm Luella Griggs," she replied, putting her cold hand into his sweaty palm.

Other news media entered the fray. Television stations from around the state converged on Brother Leadlove and the Blood of the Lamb Tabernacle. Not a night went by, it seemed, without a glimpse of the twenty-foot high plasma bottle that rose beside the sanctuary. In the past, Brother Leadlove had often bragged about the bottle, calling it an "attention getter." The bottle, appearing half-filled with a red liquid and bearing a label that read "The Blood of Jesus," now symbolized the story about Brother Leadlove and nearly always alerted the television viewer to yet another sound bite that featured a disgruntled ex-employee or ex-member of the tabernacle.

One evening, a television commentator began his report against a backdrop of the giant bottle by quipping that the large attendance prompted by the news stories meant the only person getting a transfusion these days at the tabernacle was Brother Leadlove and it was a transfusion of the green stuff and not the red. The reporter had interviewed a woman whom Brother Leadlove remembered had gotten mad and left the church because he had refused to pray for her lesbian daughter. The woman told the reporter she had given Brother Leadlove over fifty thousand dollars and it had come from the money paid her as workers' compensation following her husband's accidental death at work. When asked about the fifty thousand dollars, a spokesman for Brother Leadlove laughed and told the reporter he thought she had given more than that. The spokesman, though, did not deny that Brother Leadlove had refused to pray for the woman's daughter. "Show me in the Bible," he had stated, "where it says to pray for them kind of folks."

As the media bore down upon Brother Leadlove in the months that followed his introduction to Luella Griggs, they became fast companions. When alone, his thoughts of her competed on an equal footing with his worries. He had lots of worries now. The attorney general, who had been reluctant to act because of first amendment considerations, finally reacted to all the unfavorable publicity and had started to make noises and, worse for Brother Leadlove, inquiries.

Brother Leadlove did not surprise Luella when he confided to her a few weeks after their encounter at the altar that he, and not the church, really owned the mansion. He told her the church's executive board, which he controlled, had deeded the mansion and everything else to him after his divorce had become final. His wife, he explained, had not gotten any alimony because she was found to have committed adultery after they had separated. Detectives employed by his lawyer testified about her spending several nights at a house of a man who used to attend their church. The court had brushed aside his wife's testimony that she had needed a place to stay, that she thought it would be all right to stay with the man a couple of nights, and that nothing had happened between them. Brother Leadlove laughed about her lawyer's not bringing out that the man had undergone a prostate operation months earlier and could not have done anything even if he had wanted to.

Although Brother Leadlove's world had turned wretched, nonetheless, he now could enjoy Luella's company and, when they were apart, remember their times together. He often relived the second time he had kissed her at the altar. That was also the last time he had kissed her. She allowed him to hug her or to hold her hand, but that was all. Yet, she occasionally patted him on the shoulder or kissed him on the cheek, especially when new revelations about his wealth made the rounds. It was during those times, those discomforting times, when they seemed to draw closer together. He was so grateful she had been sent his way.

After consuming barbecued baby back ribs one evening at Au's Upstairs Eclectic, Luella's favorite restaurant, Brother Leadlove remarked, almost casually, about how he wished they could be together always. He could not believe it when she responded by asking if he had just proposed to her. He could not believe it either that he answered her by saying yes he had.

She said she would marry him but there was one condition. Because government investigators and tax auditors were now looking into his holdings and income, she feared he might lose much of what he owned and she wondered what would happen to his property if, God forbid, he wound up in jail or something. For her to marry him, she insisted, she must have security. He could better protect himself from the tax people, lawyers, and the like, she argued, if his property were in her name. So, as a condition of her marrying him and for her welfare and his own he first had to deed the mansion to her and put all his bank accounts and things in her name. Afterward, they could go to her uncle's farm a few miles north of Gaffney and a magistrate she knew could marry them.

Brother Leadlove finally agreed to her terms. They made sense, he had concluded. He did not want to wind up without anything. And he certainly did not want to lose her.

Two days later they made a round trip to the Cherokee County Probate Judge's office where they got a marriage license. On their return and against his lawyer's advice, Brother Leadlove fulfilled Luella's conditions. He deeded to her the mansion and other real property, transferred to her name his bank accounts and other investments, and delivered to her the titles of the motor vehicles.

The following afternoon they drove to her uncle's farm and parked in front of his house. She blew the horn and her uncle came out along with John Culver Walling, a local auto parts dealer and part-time magistrate. Luella's uncle stepped down from the porch, hugged her, and introduced Walling to Brother Leadlove.

"Where do you want to have the ceremony, honey?" her uncle asked.

"I think across on the other side of the pasture, in that grove of trees over yonder," she pointed.

"You sure about that, Luella," he asked. "You know, y'all can use the house or the porch. Or, we can go to the backyard where there's a pretty little trellis. It's all covered with roses."

"No, I've got my heart set on us getting married in a grove of trees and that's the prettiest grove I know of out here," Luella said.

The four walked to the grove. Tall, thick pine trees cast their dark afternoon shadows on the four as they stood beneath their green branches. The magistrate asked the relevant questions and pronounced them husband and wife. Brother Leadlove bent down and kissed his bride's clenched lips.

That evening after dinner they returned to the motel in Gatlinburg where they had checked in earlier. No sooner had they walked into their room than Luella ran to the bathroom. She complained of diarrhea. Brother Leadlove expressed sympathy for her, said he understood, and left her alone, although he had great difficulty hiding his disappointment.

Still, he thought, the day had gone well. He now had a new, beautiful wife who would help him preserve all he'd work for, no matter what the media and the attorney general tried to do to him. With her at his side, his ministry would grow and his earthly possessions right along with it. He was sure of that. He congratulated himself and fell asleep, his marriage unconsummated.

When Brother Leadlove awoke the next morning, he found Luella and the Jaguar gone.

Later that morning, Brother Leadlove rented a car, left Gatlinburg, and drove to the mansion where he spotted the Jaguar parked out front. He ran up the steps leading to the front door. He discovered its locks had been changed. He repeatedly knocked at the door, using the brass door knocker. No one answered the door.

The troubled evangelist sat waiting for his lawyer to say something, something good he hoped. "Well, Reverend," the lawyer said at last, "we've completed our investigation. I hate to tell you this, but you know that grove of trees where y'all got married at? It's not in Cherokee County, South Carolina."

"It's not?" Brother Leadlove asked.

"No, sir. It's in Cleveland County, North Carolina. A South Carolina magistrate wouldn't have any authority to marry y'all there." The lawyer shook his head. "I'm pretty sure I can get your marriage annulled. That's no problem. I can also file an action against her for fraud and deceit. What I think you'd better do, though, is what Jesus admonished litigants to do in *Matthew* five, twenty-five."

"What's that?" he asked.

"Settle."

Prue Goolsby's Recipe for Barbecued Baby Back Ribs

3 or 4 lbs. baby back ribs (2 racks)
1 c. vinegar
1 can beer
T. salt
T. black pepper
T. red pepper
water to cover
barbecue sauce (favorite brand) mixed with 1 T. liquid smoke

Cut the racks into several smaller parts. Place the parts into a large pot and add the vinegar, beer, salt, pepper, and enough water to cover the ribs. Boil for forty-five minutes. Remove the ribs from the pot and place on a baking pan. Brush barbecue sauce and liquid smoke over the ribs. Slide them under a broiler and cook the ribs about fifteen minutes and then turn them and brush again with the barbecue sauce. Continue cooking and basting the ribs until they are brown and charred on both sides. Remove the ribs from the broiler. (The ribs may be cooked on an outside grill instead of under a broiler.)

Serves: Three to four persons (make sure they understand to use their knife to cut the individual ribs from the rack parts—they'll get more meat this way and less bone and thus less dissatisfaction with the meal; have toothpicks handy, real handy).

About the Author

C. TOLBERT GOOLSBY, Jr., grew up in Dothan, Alabama, and now lives in Columbia, South Carolina, with his wife Prue. He earned an undergraduate degree from The Citadel, a law degree from the University of South Carolina, and an advanced law degree from the University of Virginia. He is a former Chief Deputy Attorney General of South Carolina. He is the author of a nonfiction work, *The South Carolina Tort Claims Act: A Primer and Then Some,* a law book published by the South Carolina Bar. His fiction has appeared in *St. Anthony Messenger* and in *Back Porch.* His first novel, *Her Own Law,* will be out soon. His Christmas short story, *The Box With the Green Bow and Ribbon,* which was published in small book form, has been turned into a play.